EVERY LAST PROMISE

EVERY LAST PROMISE

KRISTIN HALBROOK

HARPER TEEN

An Imprint of HarperCollinsPublishers

HarperTeen is an imprint of HarperCollins Publishers.

Every Last Promise
www.epicreads.com

Library of Congress Control Number: 2014952521
    ISBN 978-0-06-212128-8

Typography by Torborg Davern
15 16 17 18 19   CG/RRDH   10 9 8 7 6 5 4 3 2 1
❖
First Edition

To heroes and friends.
The real ones.

HOMECOMING

THIS IS A STORY about heroes.
I am not one of them.

SPRING

WE CAME BACK FROM spring break in Florida—me and Jen and Selena and Bean—with tans. Dark for Selena, whose skin deepened at the first sign of sun, and just a kiss of golden cream for strawberry-haired Bean. It had been, for all of us, our first trip without our parents. Earned by virtue of being four good girls with good grades and histories of good behavior.

In Florida, Jen and Selena flirted with boys whose names they hadn't bothered asking. Bean and I kept an eye on their drinks to make sure no one spiked them. We all drank tequila straight from a bottle that Selena had convinced some college guy to buy for us. Lounged on sandy beaches for hours until the hangovers passed. And then came home to lounge on the banks of a river that hadn't quite yet shed winter.

It was Saturday night. Our flight had gotten in that morning, and after a long drive to our little town hidden away like a pretty passage in the middle of a mediocre book, we were feeling lazy. But we wouldn't miss a river party.

Around us, about half of the high school, plus a few younger kids and recent graduates, had congregated. Earlier, the sun had warmed our skin, but as it set behind the hills in the distance, cold rose from the surface of the water. Selena shivered.

"I miss warmth," she said, wrapping her arms around her middle.

"Then you shouldn't have gone strapless." Jen raised a beer bottle to her lips and took a sip. She didn't shudder like I did.

"I have a sweater in my car," Bean said as the wind picked up. She bit into a grape, caught some of her own hair with it, and sputtered, picking the red strands from her teeth. "Bleh. Anyway, it's my gray Paris one."

We all knew Bean would offer, just as we all knew Selena was going to shake her head no. Selena liked to show skin.

"But yeah," Jen said. "I would go back to Panama Beach in a hot second."

A river breeze blew her long hair over her shoulder. I squinted. The party had grown, spread to the south and north of the little bank we'd settled on. Music from cars behind us competed for dancers. There were coolers of beer and Smirnoff Ice and a keg set up in the back of Steven McInnis's beater Ford hatchback. Nicole Wasserman and a few other cheerleaders waved at us as they tiptoed past on their way to their own sandbank, their sandals in one hand and their drinks in the other. A group of guys to our left erupted in laughter and high fives over I don't know what. It made me smile. All of it.

"Florida was nice, but this is home," I said.

"Oh God, don't start," Selena said.

"Our little Kayla, champion of Winbrooke, Missouri," Jen added, rolling her eyes.

"Um, we all know that title belongs to your brother." I laughed, nodding my chin at a group by the cars, where her twin, Jay, the star quarterback of our school's football team, watched his girlfriend slam beer from a plastic cup.

But I knew I was doing that crinkled-eye, sparkly-smile thing that Jen loved to make fun of whenever I started waxing poetic about this town. About long, humid summer days on the back of my horse, Caramel Star, and long, frigid winters when Conner's Pond froze over and the ice glittered like a sugar cookie as we skated over it. It was a place where heroes were real and living under the same roof as you. Superstar siblings and parents who were trusted and counted on by an entire community for their good deeds.

It was home.

We looked at the boys doing cannonballs into the river from the swimming raft anchored down in the center. When the girls lounging on the edges of the wooden boards saw us watching, they waved in our direction. Jen ignored them, but I waved back. Enough to make up for Jen, putting on her best mean girl impression. Smoothing things over was something I did often enough for my best friend. I nudged her with my elbow. "Stop being bitchy."

Jen laughed and nuzzled her head into my shoulder. "Ugh. Eve wants me to say something nice about her to Jay. One, I am not her messenger. Nor am I his. Two, if he wanted Eve, he'd go get her. Girl can't take a hint."

Beside me, Selena shifted her bare legs. Her dark hair was long enough to brush the tops of her thighs as she leaned forward. "Pretty ballsy, considering Jay's dating Bean's *sister*. Hell-*o*, like you'd do that to your friends."

I laughed. I shouldn't have laughed. It wasn't funny. It was such a little drama, but it was *my* drama. Familiar and fascinating and, in the long run, incidental. Like so much drama here.

I dropped back, crushing a patch of spring grass under my shoulders, and turned my head to look up at my friends. I stuck out my lower lip.

"Why so sad?" Jen said.

"This will all end next year," I said.

"So then enjoy it while we're all still here." Jen lowered herself onto one elbow beside me, her eyes dancing teasingly and her dimple pressing into her cheek. "You have a cricket in your hair," she said, gently plucking it out. The bug sat in her palm for a moment, then she raised her hand and it leaped to freedom.

"Thanks," I said. "What will I ever do without you?"

"What is this 'without you' nonsense? We're here now, aren't we? For another whole *year*. And after that? We'll probably apply to the same schools, be in all the same classes, ride in the same competitions together—"

"Date the same guys," Selena cut in. "Eat the same food, pee the same unicorns and rainbows—"

I snorted as Jen yanked a handful of grass out of the ground and tossed it at Selena. Half of it fell over me. I sputtered at a piece at the corner of my mouth.

"Oops, sorry," Jen said, brushing away the grass that fell on my face. "Hey, remember that time we dared Jay to eat grass?"

I remembered every prank we'd played on her brother. Every late-night brainstorming session under a blanket fort, with flashlights held under our chins to light up our faces eerily. We'd come up with some good stuff—duct-taping his toilet lid shut in the middle of the night, wrapping his car in foil before the first day of school last year—because when Jen and Jay got along, they loved each other hard. But when they didn't, they were bitter enemies. Caleb and I fought as often as siblings should, but it wasn't intense like it was with the Brewster twins. There was always an unspoken score to settle between the two of them.

"Oh my God," I said, twirling between my thumb and forefinger a stem of grass Jen had missed. "That was ages ago. He was all, 'Big deal,' and ate this massive handful. Did we ever tell him that we'd just shoveled horse poop off it?"

"I never did."

"He seriously earned those ten dollars."

"I'm going to puke," Selena said, miming retching.

"Will there ever again be someone we can mess with like that?" Jen said. "Kaaaylaaa. You're never going to leave me, right?"

I studied her pouting mouth and fluttering eyelashes. She played it off like she was joking, but Jen had been my best friend forever. The sister I would have chosen if given the chance. All our lives we've done practically everything together. I knew I wasn't the only one whose chest ached at the thought of being separated for longer than a couple of weeks.

"Of course not," I said softly. "You're the one who will be leaving *me*."

Jen made a *tsk* sound, but it was true. All I wanted was to stay here. All she wanted was to fly away forever. And I wasn't going to change my mind before college applications were due, like Jen insisted I would.

"Ladies," Bean said in her soft voice. Sometimes it sounded like she was singing. "We still have a whole *year*. Stop being all droopy and sad. Too soon."

"Yeah. Knock it off." Selena brushed off her tank top as a pack of guys watched. She had boobs to the moon and back. "Bean, what the hell is your sister letting Jay do to her?"

We all followed Selena's gaze to where Jay walked toward the river with his girlfriend, Hailey, flung over his shoulder. Her high-pitched scream rose above the other sounds. She pounded his back, but he laughed and tossed her into the river, diving in after her. When she broke the surface of the water again, she gasped for air and flung her hair away from her face. At first, she glared and raised a fist at her boyfriend, but when she looked around and realized how many people were watching her, she dropped her hand and forced a laugh.

Bean wound a piece of hair around her finger and frowned. "It didn't really look like she was *letting* him."

"They were probably just messing around," I said uncertainly. I cared less about defending Jay than I did about putting Bean at ease.

"Or maybe your brother is just a dick," Selena told Jen.

"Preaching to the choir." Jen chugged the rest of her beer and threw the bottle back toward the parked cars.

"Guys like that get away with anything." Selena shrugged.

I shot her a warning look. Not for Jen's sake—she was so over her brother's fandom in this town—but for Bean's. We didn't talk about it, but we all had heard that Jay and Hailey's relationship was full of . . . ups and downs. And over the past couple of weeks it had gotten more intense. Hailey was leaving for college that summer, but Jay was a junior, like us. I knew Jay wanted them to stay together, but Bean had told me that Hailey wanted to break it off. Waiting for their breakup was like watching the slow march of a spark to a box of dynamite.

"I'd let a guy like T. J. Brown get away with anything," I

said, nodding toward the so-hot wide receiver.

"And what, exactly, would you let him get away with?" Selena narrowed her eyes and gave me a crooked, knowing smile.

"Only gross things!" Jen yelled suddenly, blowing a raspberry into my skin. I doubled over, giggling.

Selena stood and brushed her butt off. Guys watched her do that, too. "Get a room, you two."

"You know you'd come with us," I said. "And Bean would hold the camera. Since she's the *artist*."

Bean wrinkled her nose and tossed her strawberry hair over her shoulders with both hands. "I don't even *paint* naked people."

"*Yet*. College will change that, I bet. But sorry, ladies, you're not my type." Selena tipped her head to the side and watched the people in the river. A guy who looked an awful lot like me, with dirty blond hair and a square chin, stood on the dive platform, making hooting sounds. He flung his T-shirt over his head, flexed his biceps, and kissed both of them. "Kayla's brother, on the other hand . . ."

I covered my eyes just as my brother leaped. The sound of his cannonball splash drowned out the laughter of the girls around him. "Ew, ew, ew, please don't go there."

"Caleb is a wild man tonight," Jen said.

"No more so than usual." I shrugged.

Jen pulled a stem of partridge pea by its roots and tied

the ends into a knot. She balanced the crown on my head. "Maybe. He seems pretty high-strung to me."

"'High-strung' is the definition of Caleb." I adjusted the crown so it was slightly off-kilter. "He's been going on and on with all these big thoughts about the end of high school and leaving home, lately. He almost didn't come tonight because he had 'more important things to do.'"

"That doesn't seem to be holding him back now." Bean laughed. "But . . . I don't know. I can kind of imagine how he feels, you know? All those new things waiting for him. A whole world to explore. It's exciting. Hailey's been the opposite. Doesn't talk at all about leaving. I think because of Jay. Because they haven't figured if they're going to do long-distance or not and all that."

"They better figure it out before my party because I am not having any of their drama." Jen grimaced and tied off three more flower crowns. She placed them on Bean and Selena, then finally on her own head. "The last day of school deserves nothing more than the most epic celebration."

"It will be epic," I promised. "Girls in leis, guys in grass skirts, the limbo, drinks with those cute little paper umbrellas."

"I love those," Bean said. "And the photo booth is almost done. I just need to add the sand glitter and finish cutting out the props."

"There's going to be a line out the door for that booth,

Beanie. It looks so amazing. I can't wait. Everyone is going
to be there and everyone will be talking about how *awesome*
I am."

I laughed at Jen as she raised her chin in the air and
flicked her wrist.

"Except Eve," Selena said. "She is officially uninvited."

"Aw, don't be mean, Selena." Bean gathered all four of us
into a hug. A yellow flower petal drifted down her cheek. She
blew it away with a sideways smile and pressed her forehead
against Selena's.

A strange feeling came over me. Something out of place
on a night like this. Something that reminded me of melancholy passages in books. I looked again toward my brother
splashing the girls on the platform, swimming to the shore
and getting out, shaking water from his hair. May was coming so fast. Yeah, we were all together for another year. But
I could feel a change on the air. Tiny as a single loose thread
now, but something I knew would grow, like the unraveling
of a sweater. I wanted to fight it off for as long as I could.

I loved my home. My life here. My friends. Cute boys in
sports jerseys. Horse shows. Hikes at Point Fellows, where
the view of Missouri's rolling hills and valleys went on for
miles and miles. River parties. Watching Selena flip her tiny
cheerleader's skirt at the crowds that packed our champion
football team's games. Knowing everyone. Being known.

Eventually, that would all be over.

I caught Bean's eye across our little circle. She smiled again, this time gently, like she knew what I was thinking.

"Don't worry, Jen. Your party will be tiki-riffic," Bean said. We groaned at her. "Hula-riously great? Definitely not aloha-rrible?"

"Thank God you can paint, Bean," I said as we settled back into our places in the circle. Bean stuck her tongue out at me as she got to her feet. I took a chunk of Jen's long hair and began a thin plait. Selena retrieved another drink and walked to the water's edge, still watching Caleb's antics. Bean joined her, pushing her hip into Selena's to get her attention and starting to dance. Selena put her hands in the air and moved to the beat from the stereo behind us. I moved my shoulders back and forth as I braided. Overhead, the stars winked at us.

I could have stayed sad. Thought about the day when I wouldn't have Jen's long, confident stride beside me as I walked down the school halls. When there would be no one to gossip with me on long, rambling trail rides. When the four of us lounging like this on a riverbank on a lazy weekend night would happen more often in my memory than in reality.

Like I did every time those thoughts wiggled to the surface, I stamped them back down. Because right now—this moment—was perfection.

FALL

THE BLUE HOMECOMING BANNER reaching across Main Street shimmers like the river on a stifling summer afternoon. Windless, golden warmth greets my return home. Despite the sweat beading under my arms, my sweatshirt is zipped all the way up, pulled high to hide the bottom half of my face. But even without it I would have trouble breathing.

It's been almost three months since I've been here. Home. And this late August looks the same as every August before it. Even the same face on the homecoming banner as last year. Jay Brewster has led Grant High to the state championships three years running.

We drive under the banner and I feel like I've driven into it instead. Pressing against my throat until I let out a cough. Mom glances at me in the rearview mirror, and I turn my face away from the worried wrinkles around her eyes. As the sun dips below the horizon, my breath creates a cloud on the window, and I'm glad. Because now I can't see the town I love or the people who don't want me back.

My suitcase lies open on the floor, my summer-in-the-city wardrobe spilling over the sides. Every time I start to unpack, I stop. I'm waiting for that sense of permanence, of *This is mine*, to wash over me. It hasn't yet.

"Kayla, did you get the mail?" my mom asks, drifting into the doorway as I reach under my bed, poking into the darkness that veils all manner of ancient treasures: raveling ponytail holders, too-small T-shirts, crumpled papers with bold numbers printed on them from riding competitions.

"Mm-hmm."

"Did your application packets come?"

"I think it might be too early."

"Is it?"

Under the haze of my bed skirt, her feet shift toward the stairs as her voice shifts up an octave. Her nurse's voice. The one she must have perfected when she worked in the hospital, before two kids brought her home full-time. "Well, I'm sure they'll be here soon."

It's the tone she used the day after the crash, when I finally woke from unconsciousness. *You'll be okay*, she said as I rolled into a ball, white flashes cutting through my skull. She called for pain meds to relieve my throbbing head, going so far as to suggest a specific medication and dosage to the young nurse on staff. *You'll be okay.*

My fists are clenched around dust bunnies and rubber bands when I emerge from under the bed. My hair hangs in my face, messy, a curtain that softens the reality of my mom's expectations, which are going to be dashed, I know, when I tell her and Dad that I've decided not to apply to college at all. At least, nothing beyond the community college the next town over, despite my parents' hopes, despite Jen's once-upon-a-time certainty. After being away this summer, I just don't want to leave again.

"Yeah, they'll be here soon," I mumble. Mom smiles and disappears down the hall.

I reach beneath my headboard for a sparkly notebook caught between my mattress and box spring, only a hard corner poking out, gouging a tiny hole in the paint in the wall. Unicorns and fairies and hearts drawn with glitter pens embellish the cover. My eyebrows rise with recognition. I thought this notebook was long gone, dashed away once mythological creatures began to pale in comparison to a real world of best friends and cute boys and long, lazy summer days.

The notebook is the girl I was, and so maybe that's why I cling to it. Maybe that's why I move my hand over my trash can, the notebook hovering, but pull it back quickly before dropping it in. Open to a page in the middle.

Selena kissed Lance today. She said it was like kissing a frog. Jen wanted to know how Selena knew what it was like to kiss a frog.

My notebook is a place where secrets live. If I had a pen right now, I could add one more. Instead, I stuff the note-book back under the mattress, hiding it. Hiding every secret. The way I've had to so that I can slip back into my old life.

I move across the room, light-footed with hope that I can mend the damage I've done here, and reach into my closet blindly. A paper sack crinkles, and inside, the sequins on a tank top scratch my palm. I freeze. When did my bag of stuff from that night get put in here?

Heat covers the back of my neck. I reach farther into the bag, lying to myself about what I'm certain I'll find. And what I won't find. But my fingers brush against the hard edge of truth. A cell phone. With a sharp breath, I shove the bag back into my closet and stand.

Hangers catch my ponytail and click together in a dull, thudding wood-song. I draw my hand across the back of a scratchy wool blazer. It's too small, from two years ago, but I pull it to me, pressing it against my chest. It smells like sawdust and mane oil. I hear the *clock* of hooves. My ankle aches and I flex my toes, as though I can work out the pain with a little foot stretch. As though I can forget the night my ankle was shattered.

I don't ride anymore, but that doesn't mean I can unlearn the sound of the ring. The taste of competition air. How the wind whipped through my hair as I raced across the jumping course and the way my back curved and my legs flexed taut muscles as my horse, Caramel Star, took flight over gates and walls. I always felt determined, in control, gloriously power-ful in that saddle. Like I could accomplish anything.

I wonder if it's the same for Jay. If he feels like the hero

people think he is, if every breath he takes tastes like sweet
glory and a town's adoration.

And if, on the back of his tongue, there's a faint, bitter
aftertaste of knowing someone could destroy it all.

Like me.

I wince at each rotation of the creaky bike chain in the otherwise silent night. Shop owners are home, having closed their
doors hours before. Farmers are closer to their dawn waking
than they are to their bedtimes. At the place where the small
businesses on Third Street give way to the gas stations before
the interstate, I drop my bike on the sidewalk.

In most towns, Third Street would be called Main Street
or First Avenue. It's the center of town, the pumping artery
that gives life to the farms around it. But now, at this time of
night, it's empty.

I walk to the middle of the street and stare up at the banner. The white lettering for the homecoming event listings
glows. The high school mascot is in one corner, his Roman
warrior costume frozen in mid-dance except for when the
wind blows and the fabric sways to the strains of a silent
marching band. Jay's body, in the middle of throwing a pass,
takes up a third of the banner. His face is frozen in the throes
of concentration. Beneath the helmet with the red Mohawk
painted down the center, his mouth is set in a hard line, a
muscle in his jaw clenched. His gaze focuses on something in

the distance. It's an expression that makes this town believe in something big. In the idea that determination can open doors to success. That people from little nowhere places can become great. I always did. Believed.

I stare long enough that my eyes begin to water, washing out the blinking red of the stoplight.

I cup my hands over my mouth and breathe. A sharp wind brushes my hood back from my face. Dust creates pinprick stings across my cheeks.

A bulb slowly warms to life in the back of Mackleby's Diner. Abeline Mackleby will be in the kitchen, her sleeves pushed up and her strong, round shoulders working the rolling pin on the dough for her famous sticky buns. In an hour, Third Street will smell like yeast and cinnamon and sugar. My favorite.

Since seventh grade, I've met up with my best friends on the morning of the first day of school to indulge in those huge, gooey rolls. This time, in our senior year, I won't be at that table gossiping about who will pull what pranks this year, who will hook up and who will break up, what everyone's going to wear, how we're going to crush our football opponents and how good Selena will look on the sidelines, cheering our team to victory. I don't think I'll be welcome after what happened.

I get back on my bike and go home. I sit on the porch because the house is too warm, and I think about Jen across town, her blankets kicked off her bed like she always does when she sleeps. I think about my aunt, alone in her house in Kansas City. Probably the way she likes it. Her text remains unanswered: *How's your first day back?*

I don't know how to answer her. There are too many words for a text message. There aren't enough words to fill the empty space behind the blinking bar, waiting for my response. I thought about staying in Kansas City for good. Forgetting my friends, my home, that I was popular here. Turning my back on a summer of changes as this town moved along without me. Staying far away from the guilt that eats away at my muscles. Away from what happened that night in the inky darkness behind the Brewster barn. Away from what I did, and away from what I haven't done about it.

SPRING

THE MEASURING TAPE SNAPPED closed in my palm and I called out the measurement to my dad, who wrote the number in his pocket-sized notebook. On the back steps, Caleb watched us work, his jeans and T-shirt still dusty from his morning chores.

"You could come help," I told him, "instead of just sitting there uselessly. Hold the end of the measuring tape for me."

His backward baseball cap slipped a little as he shook his head. "Who am I to take away any part of the satisfaction you'll someday feel knowing you restored that boat all by yourself?"

I climbed inside the boat frame and made a face at Caleb through the openings where some old boards had rotted away and needed to be replaced. "Dad's helping me," I point out.

"Yeah, but it was his idea to have a little daddy-daughter project."

The look of pride Dad shot me brought a smile to my face. It was only partly for me, though. The rest of it was because the boat we were working on reminded him of the sea. A place I knew he missed from his Navy days. He always wanted to get a boat but said he never had the time for one.

Three months ago, at a horse show across the state, I saw this one sitting at the edge of someone's property with a Free sign propped on the side. Lucky for me, Jen's car has a trailer hitch. My dad wasn't sure whether to grin or yell when we pulled into the yard with something that looked more like a scrap pile than a boat. All he said was that since I'd brought it home, I'd have to help make it sailable.

"And?" I said, pulling a bit of flaking paint off a board. "Are you going to tell me that once I have this thing up and running you aren't going to be begging for rides every weekend? *Kayla*"—I set the board on top of the to-keep pile and mimicked Caleb's voice—"let's go to the lake and fish. Can I borrow the boat so me and my friends can get drunk and drown ourselves in the river? Come ooonnnn." I stretched the tape out and wedged one end in the seam of two more boards, then pulled the tape even longer and shouted out that measurement, too.

"If it were that easy for drunk people to drown themselves in that river, half this town would be dead." Caleb took a long drink of the can of Coke next to him and gave me a wicked smile.

"Hey. Be nice."

"What time are you going to Jen's?" Dad cut in.

"As soon as I get one more measurement. Then I think we're ready to order the new boards."

"I'll take care of that," Dad said.

"You should have just taken the thing in to a boat shop." Caleb crushed his can under the bottom of his shoe.

"Right. Because there are so many of those around here, and we have all the money in the world," I said. "Besides, I like working on it."

I stood and crossed the yard to Dad, trading the measuring tape for the notebook, and jotted down the last of the numbers we needed.

"Almost done with *our* boat." My words were louder than they needed to be, with Dad standing right next to me. But I wanted to make my point.

Caleb laughed. "I'll help next time. Want a ride over to Jen's?"

"Sure."

I ran into the house to pull my hair into a ponytail, then back out to hop into Caleb's truck. At the Brewsters' house, I sprinted around to the rear yard, where Jen met me with an exasperated grin.

"Where have you been all day?"

I rolled up the sleeves on my shirt to avoid a farmer's tan. "Boat stuff."

"Why did I ever let you bring that rotten thing home?"

"Because you love me."

We listened to Caleb's truck roar away before I ducked into the stables to greet Caramel Star. I saddled the bay Thoroughbred my parents had gotten me for my fourteenth birthday and drew her outside to warm up. When she was ready, I planted a kiss between her eyes and climbed on her back. Jen sat tall on her striking black Trakehner waiting for me. Together, we spent the next three hours exploring the Brewster back fields, at times pushing the horses into a sprint or over a wooden cross-fence, while at other times letting them walk slowly while Jen and I gossiped.

"Did you hear Maria and Eve got into it after cheer practice Friday?" I said. "Rumor is Eve snuck into the boys' locker room to take a shower with Jared." *I* needed a shower. My hair stuck to the back of my neck.

"Wow." Jen wrapped the reins around her hand slowly. "Maria's liked him for weeks. And they just announced she's cheer captain next year. She's going to make life hell for Eve."

I shook my head. "You don't do that to your friends. And you definitely don't do that to someone who can demote you to the bottom of the cheer pyramid."

"Speaking of Eve and not doing crappy things to friends, did you hear Jay and Hailey finally broke up?" Jen said as we approached Nickerson Road.

"It's been coming. How's he taking it?"

She shrugged. "I don't know. Fine, probably. I'm just glad all that drama's done with. He's been a total asshole the past few weeks."

"He was weird at the river party during spring break. Like, pissed off but . . ." I squinted at my best friend, waiting for her to finish my thought. Which she did, like she always could.

"But trying to play it off? Yeah, I noticed that. The river dunking? What was that all about?"

"Who knows? I bet Hailey's relieved, though. The way Bean talked about how she was caught between Jay and leaving . . . I felt sorry for her."

"I felt sorry for her for ever being with Jay in the first place."

I laughed. "She was really good for him, though."

"She did make him a little more human." Jen sighed. "He'll probably go back to being the whore he was before they were together. Eve can help with that." Jen hardly had to make a motion to get her horse to stop, they were that attuned to each other. Dressage was her specialty, after all. I started to turn Caramel Star around to head back to Jen's. "Hey," she said, and I paused. "Looks like Nickerson's just been oiled." Her exasperation with Jay blew away on the breeze as her eyes lit up. A dimple dug into her cheek and she faced me. "You know what that means."

I grinned and pushed Caramel Star into a trot back to the stables.

FALL

THIS IS A MOVIE-SET kind of place.

The two bed-and-breakfasts proudly display their mentions in national travel magazines in glass frames next to their front doors. The grassy park hosts Fourth of July picnics and Easter egg hunts for boys in linen shorts suits and girls in pastel organza. Third Street shops are trimmed with tidy white wood fences and bells on their door handles. It's a dream town to raise a family in. That's what they'll tell you, at least. That's what you'll believe. The way I always have. Because it's the part of this town you can *see*.

Even in a dream town like this, a pain presses on my chest like the drop in pressure before a tornado.

I walk into Toffey's Coffees alone and set my bag on a small table, staring out the window at the streets coming to life. Aunt Bea texts again. *Did you sleep okay?*

I quickly text back yes. I don't want her to worry the way she did all those nights immediately following the accident when I kept my eyes open as long as I could at night, because closing them revealed horrors I didn't want to see. Those nights when exhaustion finally took over and I slept, only to wake tangled in damp sheets and mewling cries that brought Aunt Bea to my bedside.

I text back yes because yes is what I want to be the truth.

Erica Brewster, respected wife, mother, and county prosecutor, strides to her office building down the street. The last time I saw her, she told me she trusted me to keep an eye on everyone at Jen's party. Make sure everyone stayed safe, didn't do anything stupid. Used to be, I could be counted on for that kind of thing.

My eyelids fall in a long blink.

That relentless pressure tightens. Slowly releases with my breath.

I grab my wallet, leaving everything else at the little table, knowing that I'm drawing stares from the few customers here this early—mostly old, retired farmers who can't shake a lifetime of waking up before dawn—as I walk to the counter to place my order. Are they watching because they recognize me? Whispering to each other, *That's the girl, the one who killed that boy last spring*? The air becomes thick, like breathing underwater.

I swallow acid and scan the titles on the specialty drinks board. The Mayan Revenge isn't on the menu, and I know it. It's one of those secret-handshake types of things I know about because two years ago Caleb dated the barista who invented it. Ground cinnamon, cocoa powder, and cayenne blended with three shots of espresso, plus vanilla and almond syrups topped with milk foam. Ordering one will help me feel like I'm home. I know about something that an outsider wouldn't. A town secret.

Caleb's ex doesn't work here anymore and I wonder if the guy in front of me now knows how to make one. Noah Michaelson, a senior like me. His golden skin is darkened after a summer of working outdoors and his sandy hair hangs in his face. I know him. Have known him my whole life. His family's farm is about a mile from my place. We played together when we were little kids, but I can't remember much more than plastic wading pools and him yanking on my pigtails. He was never really part of my world after that. Especially when we got to high school. I talked to him occasionally, in passing. Once, right before Jen's party last spring. He's a quiet, odd kind of guy who is into . . . folk music. Or something. But I can't imagine that playing the banjo is the reason his biceps are gently pushing at the sleeves of his T-shirt.

When I ask if he knows how to make a Mayan Revenge, he nods while looking down at the register, examining the tip jar, checking over his shoulder at the stacks of to-go cups. Anywhere but at me.

"One of those, then. Sixteen ounces."

Noah writes my name carefully on the cup, finishing the "a" with a sharp, downward movement. The bell on the door tinkles, and I turn to see Selena walking in. She heads for a table on the opposite side of the coffee shop without even glancing in my direction. Unless I turn around and leave now, without the coffee and without my things, she will see me.

I can't hide forever. I don't want to. But I also can't brush away the fear that gnaws at the lining of my belly. The need to flee from what I did. The anxiety that I've burned my bridges and can't rebuild them. My whole life I've been like a fish in a school, surrounded by friends and family and home, until that May night, when suddenly I was caught in a fisherman's hook, dangling and gasping for air.

I want back in the water.

The sound of the milk steamer wand isn't enough to drive away the knowledge that Selena is right behind me. My ankles cross, then uncross. I lean against the counter, digging my hip into the black laminate, the seam at my jeans pocket cutting my skin.

Noah slides the finished drink to me and tucks his hair behind his ears. I pass him a five and then drop the change in the tip jar.

"Hey," he says quietly as I'm just about to turn away. His eyes rise, finally, to catch my gaze. "Welcome home."

My words lodge themselves in my throat. I inhale the cayenne sprinkled on the top of my drink's foam and that startles my senses enough to make me cough. I give Noah a small smile. Because despite the way people are looking at me, despite being afraid to see Selena, despite Noah being no one important to me, his welcome means *everything*.

"Thanks."

I take a sip of my Mayan Revenge and my lips prickle. The rush that dances through my veins gives me goose bumps before settling into a comforting, slow burn down my throat. But it's not enough to forget where I am. To stop wondering if Selena's seen me yet. What she's thinking if she has.

Selena was always Bean's best friend first, the way I was Jen's. But it was rare for any of the four of us to split that way. We all were bound together by girlish secrets told under starry skies. Who we had crushes on. Crying together over heartaches from stupid fights that never lasted long. Our dreams for what our lives would be like after we graduated. Jen talked about starting her own business and watching it grow from a big-city high-rise. Bean wanted to be an art teacher, was always joking about warping the minds of the next generation. Selena craved getting in front of the camera to give the sports report. And I always said that I would stay behind, because the idea of leaving home was unbearable. Study nursing at the community college. Always keep a spare room for when my best friends came back to visit.

I set my drink down slowly, turn, and lock eyes with Selena.

She rises out of her chair and my stomach flutters as she approaches. Her expression is carefully neutral, but that doesn't stop my smile from beginning, growing, stretching from my face down to my heart. I pick up my drink.

"Selena," I begin when she gets to the counter.

She faces the menu. And hip checks me.

I stumble backward, my heels thudding against the tile floor as I try to catch myself. My hot drink sloshes over the front of me, soaking into my shirt and searing my skin. I pull my shirt away quickly, gasping. Tears prick the corners of my eyes. I bite my tongue and battle them back. The other customers cradle their coffee mugs and look from me to their companions and back, not knowing what to do. One rises halfheartedly, then changes his mind and sits again. Selena stares straight ahead. Noah is grabbing a wet towel and heading around the counter and I think he's going to bend down and wipe the puddle on the floor but he doesn't. He holds the towel out to me.

I shake my head and leave my drink on the counter, my hand trembling so that I'm sure the mug's rattle can be heard across the coffee shop. My face burns. It is everything I can do not to cry as I move back to my table, forcing my feet not to run. A black hole opens in my chest and I want to curl into it and hide.

I stuff my things into my backpack, crushing paper, snapping the tip off my pencil because my body can't stop trembling, and push through the door. The damned bell alerts everyone to my escape. The sound rings through my head long after the bell stops moving.

Kayla Martin. Running away again.

I don't care. I hurry away. People are watching. My movements are staggered, jagged-edged like a broken window. My
shoes slam against the concrete of the sidewalk, and I wish
my skin was thicker, dense enough to not care about what I
know everyone's thinking. What they're all saying.

About the girl who killed a boy then skipped town.

A sob escapes and my shoulders quake and I can't help it.
I wish I could. I don't want sympathy.

I don't.

I want home.

I want this place so much.

But they don't want me back.

SPRING

"ALMOST FORGOT TO TELL you before, I invited Noah Michaelson to your party. Told him to bring his banjo," I said to Jen as we watched T. J. pull his truck next to Jay's SUV.

"When were you talking to him?"

"Between third and fourth. He asked me for riding photos for the yearbook ages ago and he wanted to tell me that they ended up making them a full-page spread. He's nice."

"He's a nerd. Didn't Jay beat him up in middle school?"

"Him and everyone else. But so? Everyone's coming, right?" I stepped off the porch to meet T. J. on the driveway.

"I guess," Jen said to my back.

I'd showered and changed into a T-shirt that I'd left at Jen's after our last sleepover, so I didn't feel as much like something my horse had rolled around in.

T. J. noticed. His eyes swept me appreciatively head to foot. I fought back a smile. "Mind if I ride with you?" I asked.

"Think you can handle this bad boy?" He raised an eyebrow and I laughed.

"You're talking about your truck, right?"

"Obviously," he said.

"Selena and Bean are coming together and Selena's

driving, so I'm going with you two because Selena is crazy," Jen said, slamming the front door behind her as she came out of her house. "But you have to knock off the flirting when I'm around."

"Harsh," T. J. said. "Okay, but I get to pick the music." He jangled his keys in his pocket.

"No." I flashed a playful glare at Jen. "I'll pick the music."

"Who're we still waiting on?" Jay yelled out the window. He'd already started his car, and it was filled with guys from the football team hollering for him to get going. Behind Jay, Steven McInnis had another four guys crammed in his Ford. People loved riding with Steven because he knew, completely, that his car was a pile of crap, which meant he held nothing back on the slick gravel.

Just then, Bean's car rounded the corner in the distance, with Selena at the wheel. Bean never drove during joyriding, and Selena didn't have a car but loved driving, so they traded places on nights like this. Bean was belted in and shrank down in the passenger seat and Selena whooped it up out her window as the Honda approached.

"Just Pete and whoever he's bringing, but he'll have to meet up with us there. I'm tired of waiting," Jen hollered back as I slid across T. J.'s seat. Jen pushed in after me. She slammed the door shut and grinned. Her light brown hair was covered with a turquoise cowgirl hat. "Giddy up, pardner."

T. J. hopped back in and fired up the old truck. We

peeled out of the driveway after Jay and Steven. Selena and Bean sped toward us, bringing up the rear. A quarter mile past Jen's house, we took a right and headed out to the gravel county roads. Just as Jen said, there was machinery out there and bright orange Fresh Oil warning signs on the sides. The workers had gone home for the day and we were out here alone.

I rolled the truck radio dial between my fingers, honing in on a rock station through the static.

"Why don't you ever replace that radio?" Jen said, putting the window up so her hat didn't fly off her head.

"It's vintage," T. J. said. I snorted. But I loved this old truck. Its half powder-blue, half red-brown-rust paint job, the long crack running across the bottom of the windshield, even the manual door locks. The way the guy driving it fit the whole image, with his perfectly faded T-shirt and jeans.

"Yeah, right," Jen said. "I'm just hoping we don't break down out here because Jay's car is going to stink with all those boys in there, and I do *not* want to ride home with him."

"There is a well-loved machine under this hood," T. J. said.

Jen rolled her eyes. "Pull your machine over. Jay's going first."

T. J. took the truck to the side of the road behind Steven's Ford and let the engine idle. We watched Jay's SUV pick up speed, then, with a suddenness that slammed bodies against doors, launch into a doughnut. The guys inside yelled and stuck their heads out the windows as they spun. When the car stopped, Jay returned to the middle of the road and shot off into the dark for a second spin on the next stretch of road. Steven pulled his car out and followed Jay's tracks, his car spinning, catching enough air to spin on two wheels for a split second. When they landed, his passengers pounded their fists on the roof of his car.

Then we were up.

T. J. pulled out. His foot pressed harder on the gas. The truck bellowed in response, pushing our backs against the seat as we went faster and faster. My pulse pounded with the thrill of sixty, seventy, seventy-five miles per hour. Gravel flew up behind us, blurring my view of Selena and Bean in the rearview mirror. When we got close to the spot where Jay and Steven had spun out, I needed air.

"Trade with me!" I said to Jen.

I flung my body over Jen and she skidded underneath me. Our limbs knotted up for a brief moment, but then we were free again and she was fixing her hat. I clutched the window crank and pumped. As the window lowered, cool air—the temperature caught somewhere between winter and summer—filled the cab.

Before I could think too much about it, I grabbed the edge of the truck roof and hauled myself through the window to sit in the doorframe. My heart pounded in my shoulders and neck. In the distance, the soft lights of my hometown glimmered. The heady scent of hot oil filled my nostrils, lying heavy in my lungs.

"Kayla!" Jen screamed. A light on the dashboard illuminated her face with green. "I'll kill you if you fall!"

"Hold on to her legs," T. J. yelled, not looking from the road, his face screwed up with concentration. I felt Jen's arms wrap around me. Wind whistled around my upper body, filling my ears with so much sound I almost couldn't hear Jen's uncontrollable laughter or the shocked screams coming from the other cars.

My long blond hair whipped around my face and neck, the rushing air pricked at my skin. I felt free, like I was soaring. With my chin tipped back, I saw a black sky full of pin-drop stars. They were so still, the enormous backdrop of them, and I was moving so fast. Blood rushed to my head as I threw it back farther, exposing my throat to the night.

"Spinning!" T. J. hollered.

On cue, my hands gripped the truck as tightly as I could. T. J. turned the wheel and, like magic, his tires caught on enough oil to send us spiraling across the gravel. But I felt weightless. Floating. I closed my eyes against the beautiful dizziness that was building inside me. Car horns honked their approval. Inside the truck, Jen still laughed. With her holding my legs, I was secure. Safe. And even if I did slip from her grasp, the blanketing sky above me, I knew, would catch me as I went flying out of the truck. Would cradle me gently. In a moment that felt like time had stopped for me, that nothing bad could ever happen to me, not in this town, not with these people holding me tightly to them, I let go of the truck, raising my palms to the air, and shouted my joy to the sky.

FALL

KANSAS CITY BUSTLES. IT is a place with noise and concrete and highways made up of more than two lanes, and Aunt Bea lives on a street where the houses face off from one another across streets where lawns are square and tidy. I already knew that I was a small-town girl, born and bred and content to stay there. I couldn't hear in that city. Couldn't think. Breathe. When my sleep wasn't full of nightmares, I dreamed about land that went on forever and how an autumn sunset over the fields contained a thousand shades of orange and gold.

When I woke, sweating, I remembered that I was hundreds of miles away from home in a room that was stark, without anything that could identify it as mine: competition trophies, half-used cakes of eye shadow, photos covering more of the mirror than they let through—of me and my friends, me sitting tall on my horse, me against the backdrop of the river or an endless turquoise summer sky.

Hundreds of miles and a million worlds away from home.

Mom drives me to school on the first day, those lines of worry I'm getting used to deep around her eyes. I haven't been behind the wheel of a car since May. Thinking about it makes my muscles seize.

I stand in the doorway to first period math class and stare at the empty desk next to Pete Sloan, uncertain if it's the seat I should take. It's in the middle of the room and all around him are people. *My* people. Once upon a time. My old friends, the ones who would cluster around me to defend me from anything the world could throw at me. Even Pete, who was never anyone special to me. Just another guy on the football team. Last year, I would have taken that center-of-it-all seat without a second thought.

Now, my old friends see me and quickly turn away or stare too long, challenge or disgust pooling in their eyes. I fight back tears. I fight back the inclination to run. Again.

I nibble the tip of a pen then draw myself up to every bit of my five-seven height, cross the room, dump my bag on the desk next to Pete, and slide into the seat, focusing on a hang-nail on my left hand like it's the most interesting thing I've ever seen. Pete's stopped talking to the person sitting on the other side of him and I know he's looking at me, his brows drawn together, perplexed.

"Jesus." He draws it out. "You're back."

It's better than the other things he could have said.

"I am." I'm back. I'm here. In this school, in this class, in this seat in the middle of the room. With everyone staring at me, my skin crawling, trying not to choke on the lump in my throat.

He stares at me for a few seconds. An uncomfortably long time. Is he mapping the face of a killer? Is he wondering if saying anything else to me would taint him?

"I'm saving that seat for T. J.," he says, glancing to the front of the room as though seating assignments are written on the board.

"Oh. Sorry." For some reason, my body doesn't want to move, and I realize I crave talking to someone I used to know. Our conversation spikes a high that I'm scared to come down from. It's a taste of the girl I used to be, the one who was friends with everyone, the one without a care in the world.

But he stares at me as I twist the pen again, grinding it against my lips. I want to pull my arms in close to my sides, my knees to my chest, become too small to see. But I need to spread out, claim space. Tell everyone, *I'm here. I'm not leaving again.*

Pete leans across the aisle toward me. Every breath I take is air filled with his scent: boy sweat and grass. He says something, but I have no idea what it is because my ears are suddenly buzzing. My chest plummets and I lean forward to hide my need to breathe like a girl trapped under dark river water. Every morning until graduation, I will see these people in my first period class, in second period, in third.

How long until I stop feeling this way?

I turn back to Pete, my temples throbbing, and interrupt whatever he was saying. "I'll move. Don't want to take T. J.'s seat."

His eyebrow twitches. I jump to my feet and snatch my backpack as T. J. trips through the doorway and spies me at his desk.

"No way, she's back?" His voice travels across the room. A chorus of noise—coughs, incomprehensible words—rises behind me. Does he even remember that night we spun in his truck, the hundreds of flirtatious one-liners he had tossed my way? "Killer Kayla. Ha. I didn't even have to work for that one."

I meet Pete's eyes again. They've softened around the edges. He frowns, looks at T. J. and back at me, hesitating. As though he doesn't want to agree with T. J. but doesn't want to stand up to him, either. The misshapen bones in my ankle seize and I swallow back a rise of emotion. "Don't—never mind."

I spin away from the desk and sit at another empty one in the far row. I hope I haven't taken someone else's spot.

Killer.

As though I had intent.

Bean is in the seat across the aisle from me. I see her and my mouth tastes like sawdust, like the dry air at a horse meet. I want my horse near me now so I can climb into the saddle and escape. Seeing Bean makes me forget why I came home. Makes me scared of the things I know, things I've witnessed. She peers at me, her wide eyes seeming to convey some secret message that I refuse to pick up. She looks different somehow. All color and no form. A cloud of red, a wall of green. Paler than usual but her cheeks and lips brighter, like a slushy spilled on snow. But Bean never wears makeup and I can't look at her, flushed like that.

"Hi," she whispers.

I look around the room at everyone pretending not to see me.

"Hi," I say, letting my eyes stop on the whiteboard.

My tongue trips over the words I want to say—*I missed you, I have questions I don't want the answers to*—so instead of talking I take out a piece of paper, unfolding and smoothing it on the tabletop so that I look like I have something to do. I look up to see Pete still staring at me, turned around in his seat, his sharp-jawed face softened with a mixture of curiosity and sadness, and I don't want it.

Selena walks into the classroom and I sink down in my seat. Even when we were friends she had an edge. A personality that rolled like a pot of boiling water. Moods that changed with every pop of a bubble. But she was always loyal to her friends. I was hoping, maybe, she might have moved on from hating me for what I did.

But of course she hasn't. I've never tested her loyalty like this before. No one has. And now I know there's a line. A limit.

When she spots me, Selena pauses between me and Bean.

"You really *are* back," she breathes.

"I'm back." There is too much hope in my voice. She pounces on it.

"You should have stayed away. Nobody wants you here."

I know. And knowing makes my next breath catch low in my lungs so that I have to strangle it out. I hate faltering in front of Selena and Bean and everyone else staring at us. In another world, these are the moments we would have watched other people have, the ones that would sustain gossip for days at a time. I never imagined I would be at the center of those stories.

Bean rubs at a spot on her desk with her thumb. Listening but slouched over the wood. Hiding.

"You'd better move along, then," I say. My voice is tight. I bite the inside of my mouth and remind myself that I'm the one in the wrong. I'm the one who ran. I'm the one who killed a boy. And now, instead of begging for my friends back, I'm pushing them further away. I take a slow, deep breath and hold my hands toward her, palms open. "Look, Selena—"

"Don't," she cuts me off abruptly. Selena's eyes shift.

When she sees the approval in the faces of our classmates, her voice rises. "You did a horrible thing. I can't even talk to you."

She walks away and I stare at my desk as talking rises again in the classroom. Selena says the things she's supposed to. The words that prove she's on their side, not mine. But she's not wrong. I *did* do a horrible thing. I look away. Catch Bean's eye again, finally. Her neck is covered with red splotches. It's not exactly strange, the way she's sitting there quietly while Selena says these things to me. Bean never teased or mocked anyone. It isn't like her. But that she's not pulling Selena away, telling her to stop being mean or even that I'm not worth their effort?

She's acting like Selena isn't her best friend.

She's acting like they don't even know each other.

Bean looks at the floor. Her fingernails pick at a fraying thread at the hem of her shirt. Her spine curls, like she can make herself smaller. Like she can disappear.

The pen in my fist scribbles a tiny oval on my paper, through my paper, drilling a tiny hole in my desk. The manic doodling is the only way I can keep my hands from shaking.

My head remains lowered until the sound in my ears dies down, my brain wills my chest to rise and fall slower . . . slower . . . slow enough that they can't tell if I'm still breathing, how I'm feeling, if I feel anything at all. Numbness, when it settles over me, is a relief. I fold the paper into tiny squares, hoping the passing minutes cause everyone to forget what they just heard Serena tell me.

My parents call what happened an "accident" so much that even I've started to believe them, believe that it was all something that I had no control over.

Coming home means I have to tear the word "accident" apart and face the ripped-edge truth of each little piece, whatever that is. I stash the square of paper away as class starts. When I finally look up, I'm startled to find Bean watching me.

"It must be weird," she whispers, and the way she's looking at me, intently, and the way her back is straight again, her body leaning toward me, make me realize that she's not trying to avoid *me*. She's looking for something. What? No, I know what, in a way. But what . . . *exactly*? I can't meet her eyes. I don't want to know the exact thing, so instead I connect the freckles on the bridge of her nose like they are constellations. "Weird . . . not remembering something that happened to you."

The sheriff might have been camping in the hospital hallways, the way he showed up in my room only moments after I woke up from the accident the day after it happened. He asked questions, and I answered them as best I could. My best wasn't very good. Scenes from the night before were an aching jumble. I was honest then, telling him the events were mostly in a fog. He was understanding. Patted my hand, made some comment about oiled gravel, and wished me a quick recovery before he left.

"Memory loss is weird," I say, twirling my pen between my fingers.

"Do you think you ever will? Remember?"

"The doctor said it is possible."

"When?" Her fingers aren't rubbing anything anymore. They're clutching to the sides of her desk. "I mean, if it comes back."

"It's hard to say. Brains take time to heal."

"But it *will* heal," she says.

"I don't know." I shift to the left and look exaggeratedly toward the front of the room, but the teacher is arranging piles of books and doesn't seem to care about the pockets of chatter throughout the room.

Bean makes a noise in the back of her throat and pulls her hair forward, over her shoulder. I expect her to twirl a piece around her finger or comb it absently, maybe, things she would have done months ago while we had a conversation, but she doesn't. She just holds the thickness of it in her fist. As though it steadies her. She frowns. "That must be frustrating."

"Frustrating," I repeat. "Yeah."

She releases her hair. Her voice softens. "Sometimes things happen for the best. Maybe not remembering . . . is a good thing."

My pulse begins to speed up. Because if she's saying I

shouldn't remember what happened that night, it means there's a possibility that I'm doing the right thing by coming home, by keeping my secrets. That even though I've stayed silent because I've wanted to, I'm not the only one.

Then again, Bean is exactly the kind of person who would keep bad things secret, if just to spare anyone else the trouble of dealing with them. Is that what's happening here? If so, that means I'm a certain kind of person. Not just a girl who kills. A girl who lets others fall on swords for her.

That's not who I want to be.

But I'm scared to ask and find out for sure.

"Maybe I will remember. Sometime."

Bean's entire body perks up.

"But maybe not. Brains are weird." I jab the tip of the pen into the cover of my textbook. *I just want to come home.*

Bean deflates again. "I'm sorry, Kayla. This is probably upsetting you."

"Yeah . . ." I tug on a strand of hair. She doesn't know why it's upsetting to me. Not *all* of the reasons. But then she doesn't know what I know—remember—either, which is everything. And that makes me question who should be more upset, between the two of us.

I have to move the conversation away from that night. To anything else. I take the book Malcolm Hart passes over his shoulder back to me, open it, and pretend to read the intro. "Precalc is supposed to be pretty hard, right? And Mr. Klein is a beast. Not looking forward to it."

Bean bites her lip and looks down, a sheen of disappointment covering her features. But I push it out of my mind and start taking notes.

Yeah, I was honest when I woke up at the hospital.

Less so now. But is telling Bean that I remember clearly what happened that night the right thing to do? Or does she want to bury it, pretend it never happened, as much as I do?

I get through my next two classes, keeping my head down, only speaking when I absolutely have to, before I see them. The figures, siblings, standing by my locker are as familiar as anything else at home. Jay Brewster in his letterman jacket, Jen Brewster with her brown hair trailing down her back. Her shirt is new, the straps rounding over strong shoulders, but her fitted jeans are old. Perfectly faded. A year ago, it's an outfit we would have planned together. Now, she looks me up and down, taking me in without a change in her expression. She is unreadable. I don't know what Jen's thinking—something that would have been impossible last spring—because, unlike everyone who had something horrible to say to me after the accident, Jen had said nothing. No texts, no emails, no calls. That was the worst thing that could happen between us.

And Jay . . . His lips press together. His grasp on his backpack is tight. What is going through his head, facing the girl who killed one of his friends? The girl who knows the terrible things he's capable of. He nods once in my direction, but not quite *at* me, then walks away.

But Jen. She waits for me to approach her, her features hard like rock, bringing a rush of white noise to my ears. It's the same buzzing that follows me around since that night last May, the same sounds I just heard in first period math: crinkling metal, hot rain on pavement. Gravel falling back to earth.

She doesn't approach me but waits for my footsteps to find her.

I've told Jen Brewster that she's my best friend a million times. I've drawn thousands of hearts on notes we've passed. Once, I told her that I didn't know what I'd do without her.

For months, I was without her, and I was scared she was back here despising me with the same intensity that I loved her.

Love her.

I try to anticipate what's going to come out of her mouth, but I have no idea what Jen will say. There's nowhere for me to turn, and I swear I won't run away again.

I fumble for a word, for the right words. But nothing comes. I stop at my locker. Tuck my fingers under the strap of my bag.

"You came back," Jen says.

I can't tell if she is angry or curious or condescending or

happy. And that's not me and Jen. I used to be able to know what she was thinking with barely a glance. I feel ill.

"Yeah." The word is husky, filled with unshed tears. "How have you been?"

Her mouth twitches and I can hear what she doesn't say: *Who are you to ask that question?* Instead, "I heard you were back in town. Weird."

My heart drops to my feet, crushes. She's not even being mean about it, and there's not a trace of bitterness. She's controlled, matter of fact. There's *nothing*.

"I'm back."

I glance at the people walking past us, staring, not bothering to hide their interest in my conversation with Jen. They want a first-day-of-school scene to talk about. I know, because I would have wanted the same thing last year. Now I want our scene to disappear into the wall.

"I heard you were in Kansas City. Nice there?"

I swallow. "It's different."

"But it must've been nice. After everything. To go somewhere different."

"I needed . . ." What did I need that wasn't obvious, that she doesn't already know? "To come back."

"I thought your leaving was a good idea."

I clutch my bag to my shoulder, refusing to let it slide down my arm the way I want to slide down these lockers.

She shifts. Less than an inch. A microscopic movement

of the bottom of her shoes, a twitch in her ankle. Something only someone who *knows* her would see.

"Jen . . ." Why is it so hard to say it? *I missed you.* But my tongue dances around the syllables, ties itself like a sailor's knot on the "I" and won't let go. This vulnerability with Jen is new. Unwelcome. Terrifying.

Jen's line of vision shifts to a spot over my shoulder and her eyes narrow. I turn slowly, not knowing what to expect. Bean stands several feet back, watching us, one hand reaching into her locker.

"See you around," Jen says to the back of my head.

When I twist back to face her, she's already moving away. "Wait—"

"No, Kayla. I had to wait for you. Now, you can wait for me."

I stand there in the hallway, watching her back. An arm slams into my shoulder and there's laughter. A random voice I don't recognize mutters, "Killer Kayla."

Killer.

Like I did it on purpose.

Which . . . I had.

SPRING

THE FOUR OF US snuggled under layers of blankets, our fingers greasy with buttered popcorn. Selena had been talking for fifteen minutes about how, since we were almost seniors, she was only dating college boys from now on. Bean rolled her eyes toward me and we shared a secret, patient smile, our hair mingling across our pillows like eddies of yellow and red. Jen licked her fingers clean of butter and perused the bottles of nail polish I'd brought down from my room.

"Steven McInnis had the balls to text me last night," Selena said. "At, like, one a.m. Like I'm a booty call? I don't even know how he got my phone number. Loser."

"He was with Jay last night," Jen said. "Jay was probably drunk and gave it to him."

"Why do they even hang out together?" I said. Steven McInnis wasn't that well-liked, except for when he was with Jay.

"The great football brotherhood," Jen said. Her voice lowered dramatically and she waved her hands in the air. "Once, they would have gathered naked in great Roman coliseums and wrestled to the death. Bloodbaths of honor. Now, they hide under layers of padding and throw a stupid ball across a field."

"Shame how things have changed. They used to get all oiled up, too," Selena said over our laughter. "Gleaming muscles. Ooh yes. Now we're lucky if guys don't smell like hogs."

I snorted. "You watch too many gladiator movies. I'm pretty sure those ancient guys were ripe, too. Deodorant wasn't invented back then."

"Lucky for girls back then, body spray wasn't invented, either. I hate when guys douse themselves in that stuff. Yuck." Jen shoved a handful of popcorn in her mouth and unscrewed a bottle of nail polish.

"I prefer a little smelly to oily and naked." Bean wrinkled her nose. "But mostly, I wouldn't want to see their . . . *things* flinging all over the place when they wrestled. *Ew.*"

"Your imagination is lacking." Selena giggled and reached over me to tickle Bean in the ribs. "I just wouldn't want to see the junk of anyone around here. But gladiators? Oh yes. Give me a real man any day."

"Blah, blah, college guys. Yeah, we've heard it before. This town isn't a complete wasteland of boys," I said, shoving Selena back in her place. A half-popped kernel stuck in my teeth and I paused to dig it out.

"Are you talking about T. J.?" Selena said. "Hotness is not everything."

"Works for now." I shrugged. "Not like I'm trying to find my soul mate and settle down or anything."

"What about Jay? I can imagine him in some kind of

gladiatorial combat," Selena said.

Jen scowled at the way her nail polish brush skipped across her finger messily. "Can we not talk about my brother and oil at the same time? I'm going to puke."

"You two would be cute together," Selena continued, nudging Bean. "He keeps sitting next to you at lunch."

"Seriously?" Bean gave Selena an incredulous look. "He just barely broke up with Hailey. It's like second degree of separation spit swapping."

"Gross," I agreed.

Jen blew on her nails to dry them and looked at us. Saying nothing.

"This town needs some new blood." Selena sighed. "Did you happen to invite anyone I don't know to your party, Jen?"

"I invited everyone who matters." Jen frowned at her nails and reached for a cotton ball to wipe off the red polish.

"So, same old, same old, then," Selena said.

"There are some nice guys around here," Bean said. "What about Noah Michaelson? Didn't you say you invited him, Kayla?"

Selena pulled her shoulders a few inches off the floor so she could give Bean the evil eye. "He's weird. Does he ever say a word to anyone? I don't think you actually love me anymore."

"You're one to talk. Didn't you just suggest Jay—" She broke off, her smile fading and her glance flicking up at Jen.

"Oh Jesus," Jen said, choosing a new nail polish color. "It's not like I don't know the truth about my own brother. Even if he wasn't my brother, I'd never date him."

That strange, heavy silence fell over us again. Selena finally broke it by grabbing the remote and pointing it at the TV. "This movie is crap. Let's dance."

The quick inhale of air the rest of us took left me light-headed for a moment. I ran upstairs for my laptop and put on my dance playlist, then sat on the couch next to Jen and slowly unscrewed the cap to the glittery gold polish.

I thought about the time I'd had a crush on Jay Brewster. I was probably ten or eleven and he was just starting to form muscles in his scrawny arms. He'd so far avoided the awkward phase it seemed every other boy our age was going through and looked poised to dodge it completely. But my infatuation had faded quickly. Even then, Jay Brewster knew he was something special, and his ego's growth spurts matched his body's.

When Hailey first started going out with Jay last fall, we'd thought it was strange. Jay usually dated girls who worshipped him, but Hailey wasn't the kind of girl to have patience for diva types. She was Bean's older sister, and we all looked up to her as an example of independence and strong will, staying at the top of her class all throughout high school, getting into big-name schools, leading the field hockey team in goals. Over the past year, Jay had mellowed a little bit, though. Her influence seemed to be good. Until the weeks leading to their breakup.

Once, back in February, I came down Jen's stairs to over-hear Jay telling Steven that he always got what he wanted. And Steven agreeing with him. Who could stop boys like them? They'd laughed. I'd brushed it off then. It was easy to talk big. Nothing to take seriously.

Still, I'd felt compelled to grab the cookies I'd come down for and hightail it back upstairs, crossing my arms over my chest because I was wearing a fitted T-shirt and no bra underneath.

In my living room now, Selena flung her head and arms around to the music. Her reaction to bralessness and boys was different than mine. She'd given me a flippant *I don't care* earlier in the evening when I'd mentioned that my brother was home and so she might want to wear more than a sports bra and boy shorts, but I knew she cared very much because her eyes roved from the front door to the stairs to the kitchen as though waiting for him to come in and see how beautiful she was.

He was almost a college guy, after all.

I always liked watching Selena and Bean dance. They were so different. Selena looked like she should have been dancing on a stage at a club. But Bean moved like she heard a dif-ferent song than the rest of us. Her movements were a little off-tempo, slower. In one moment, Bean reminded me of a little girl. But then I blinked and she swung her hip to the left and she looked so confident that she seemed impossibly far away, older, closer to womanhood than the rest of us. More like the woman Bean's real name, Sabine, suggested. Even though she was the only one of us four who was still a virgin.

I drew the polish brush along my thumbnail and thought again about our one year left to be together in this town. How I wanted to make it special. Sometimes, it felt easy to figure out who everyone else was in our group. Jen, our leader. Selena, the warrior. Bean, the peacekeeper. But me?

Across the room, my most recent competition ribbon sat on the mantle above the fireplace. A huge, ruffled blue thing that I hadn't yet taken to Caramel Star's stall to put with the other ribbons and cups I'd collected over the years. Jen had taken first in dressage but hadn't placed in the top three in jumping. I'd congratulated her, and she'd said, "We did all right, but I just can't get off the ground like you can. You're so much stronger than me. Better grounded in your saddle."

And maybe that was me. Strong and grounded. I knew, somehow, that after high school, I was going to be the one to keep us close. I was going to be the one to insist we come together, insist they come home regularly and reconnect with one another. Without that, I was afraid the four of us would drift apart.

But we never would. I'd make sure of it.

FALL

WHEN MY FIRST DAY back at school finally ends, I wait for the bus several feet away from the little groups of two and three students, my collar drawn up, my shoulders hunched to my ears even though it's sweltering. My fingers search for fuzz in my pockets.

I stare at Ulysses S. Grant High School to avoid looking at the people around me. To avoid meeting their eyes. Guessing what they're saying because none of them bother covering their mouths with their hands as they gossip about me. T. J.'s so-clever "Killer Kayla" has spread. At first, I wanted to puke every time I heard it. From my old friends. From people I barely know. But now my ears have started tuning it out like background noise.

It's just a beginning, I know. I fluctuate between feeling slowly destroyed and feeling almost buoyed by their actions, as though their words are a penance I have to weather before I can belong again.

I have three classes with Jen and Jay Brewster. Three hours each day to sit in the back corner and pretend to be invisible while people glance over their shoulders every few minutes to check up on me. Three hours to watch her talk and laugh with her friends—our friends—and watch him give teachers lopsided grins when they reprimand him for talking over their first day of school syllabus reading. Even the ones who frown at him give a reluctant pass. Boys will be boys, and Jay, he's a star in whose orbit everyone shines a little brighter.

Bean stands on the school's front lawn, in front of the boulder engraved with a picture of the mascot, with another girl, someone I don't know, who might have moved here over the summer or is bused in from one of the four towns surrounding ours. I'm not sure if her new friendship makes me happy for Bean or sad. For her, for me. For Jen and Selena. She seems to feel my eyes on her because she looks away from the other girl, and her expression as she faces me is different from everyone else's. There's no hostility. Nothing to read in her eyes, her mouth, her stilled body language.

I watch Bean for too long. My thoughts form questions I've gotten good at ignoring. For a moment, I wonder if she's thinking the same thing I am: *What does she know? What does she remember?* I tuck the possibility away in a corner of my mind and turn away from the school to face the highway.

I grip my bag tighter. With my other hand, I tuck a piece of hair behind my ear, finger my shirt collar, and finally, rest my hand stupidly by the top of my thigh.

I jump when a voice sounds in my ear. Noah Michaelson

stops next to me. "Why are you standing here all alone?"

He doesn't seem uncomfortable to be talking to the school pariah. I study his face: golden skin across high cheekbones, dark, almond-shaped eyes, lips set in a serious line. His dad's white and his mom's Filipina. I recall he spent a year during elementary school in the Philippines with his mom. When he came back, he was different. Something was different. But I didn't see him enough anymore to put my finger on what. When I don't answer his question, he rummages through his backpack, pulling out a candy bar.

"Twix?" he says.

"I'm okay," I say.

Noah looks over at the school mascot boulder. When he starts to stuff the candy bar package in his pocket, I fiddle with my sweatshirt zipper and begin to turn away, my chest stinging more than I want it to from our three-second exchange.

"Glad to be home?" he says.

I squint down the road, searching for the telltale yellow of the school bus. "I don't know."

I'm not sure what compels me to be honest with Noah Michaelson. Maybe it's the way he approached me, first. Or how he didn't call me Killer Kayla. Or how we're both kind of outcasts now.

"It's good to see you again," he says.

I'm glad my face is half obscured by my collar because

my chin trembles when he says it. I swallow back a lump and can't answer him.

The candy wrapper crinkles again. Noah's dark eyebrows are drawn, but then he looks up at me from under his lashes and gives me a weak smile.

"Thanks," I finally say. I scan the crowd around us, my glance falling, again, on Bean. She's still watching me and something inside me twists. I adjust my bag strap on my shoulder as the bus approaches. "See you later, Noah."

"Yeah."

I climb onto the bus, relief taking over when I spot an empty seat. I fall on the bench and look out the window. Noah waves his Twix at me as the bus pulls away from the school.

SPRING

I WAS UP EARLY the Sunday morning before school was out for the summer. I raced through my chores. It was already getting hot, and the glare of the sun made me squint as I headed back to the house. Dad was filling his coffee mug in the kitchen as I passed through on my way to the stairs.

"How's it going with the new boards?" He replaced the coffeepot and picked his baseball hat off the counter.

"Pretty good. They're looking watertight since we re-bent that wonky one, but I won't know for sure until she gets on the water. All that's left now is sanding and painting. We should have her in the river by the end of June."

"Can't wait. Better think of a name before then."

I paused. "Me?"

Dad fitted his hat on his head and nodded. "You brought her home—"

"For you," I interrupted.

"—and you've worked hard to get her in shape. I think you should do the honors." Dad flashed me a smile as he headed back outside, sidestepping Mom as she walked into the kitchen.

"Are you going upstairs? Will you tell Caleb to put his laundry away instead of throwing it on his floor, please?

We're leaving for the Pattersons' in a hour."

I nodded, but my thoughts were on boat names. The *Farmer's Daughter? River Drifter?* "Will do."

Upstairs, Caleb lounged on his bed, finishing his homework. His clean socks were balled up and scattered across his floor.

"Mom said put your clothes away. Slob."

"I will later. Have to finish this."

I peered at the notebook he was writing in. "Homework? I'm done with that for the year."

"No, not homework, dummy. I was done with that the moment my acceptance letter came." He made a mark on the piece of paper without looking up at me. "This is my list of girls who might be lucky enough to get some of this hot, hot Caleb action before I leave this summer."

I picked up a sock ball at my feet and threw it at his head. "Gross."

"You say gross, but I've seen the way your friend looks at me. No one can resist all this." He grinned and tossed the sock ball back in my direction. I spun out of the way.

"Stay away from my friends," I called over my shoulder as I headed for the shower.

Caleb jumped out of the car before it had really come to a stop, raced across the yard, tossed Bean's little brother, Eric, over his shoulder, and hauled him to the trampoline out back. Easy to do, since Eric was the smallest fifteen-year-old I knew, even though he promised everyone he came into contact with that his growth spurt would come soon. And then they'd be sorry.

I met Bean on the porch, handing her the peach pie I'd baked.

"Brothers," I said.

"Caleb's his favorite person in the world," Bean said. "It'll suck when he leaves for college."

"Not for me. The house will be way less stinky."

Bean laughed and we went into her house to set the pie on the kitchen counter before heading to the back deck. Ever since my mom had delivered Bean's older sister, Hailey, a couple of months before Caleb was born, she and Bean's mom had been good friends. When the weather was good, our families would get together around a table groaning with food. The adults reminisced about simpler times while we shuddered at the idea of a world without the internet. Today, with the heat of late spring soaked into the ground, Bean's dad was cooking burgers on the grill.

I grabbed a can of Orange Crush from the cooler at my feet and popped the tab, peeking over his shoulder at the meat sizzling over coals, then at the spread on the wooden picnic table behind him. I turned back to Bean. "What are you going to eat?"

"Potato salad and pie, I guess," Bean said. "My mom

went to the store last night and goes, 'Bean, since you don't eat meat, I'll pick you up some chicken, okay?'" Bean rolled her eyes. "They don't get it."

I laughed and followed Bean over the backyard's wooden pole fence and out into the fields, stepping carefully to avoid cow pies. "Ah, Bean, our favorite town oddball."

"And that's okay with them when it comes to almost everything else. 'Want to do art? We'll convert the barn loft into a studio for you!' 'Want to go vegetarian? Here, eat chicken. It's not meat, right?'" She threw her hands in the air and shook her head. "But Eric doesn't mind. He gets to eat all the leftovers."

"I'll eat your burger tonight, Bean," I said.

"Yeah. Thanks."

"Here to help."

Bean slid the barn doors open. I climbed the ladder to the loft and flopped on the futon across from her easel. The canvas propped up there was unfinished. Something like a landscape, I thought, but in unlikely colors. Magenta and teal. I peeked out the window, noticing echoes between the way the land rolled outside and the way the landscape in Bean's painting did in front of me.

"How's Hailey doing?"

"Fine. She should be home from work any second. She just gave her two weeks' notice." Bean picked up a brush and tapped it against the side of a jar. The smell of solvents drifted to me lazily. I grabbed the patchwork pillow next to me and put up my feet.

"I thought she was staying for the summer."

Bean dabbed the brush on a rag and reached for her palette. She shook her head. "She's nannying for a family in South Carolina in June and July. Decided she could use the extra money. She is so ready to get out of here."

"I don't get it."

"I know you don't," Bean said. "Sometimes I can't imagine leaving, either. Other times, I can't wait to go. Just depends . . . I don't know. On how restless I'm feeling, I guess."

"It's so beautiful here." Through the skylights above my head, I watched the sky slowly change colors. A little bit of violet. A little bit, even, of that magenta Bean had used in her painting.

"There are lots of beautiful places in the world." Bean examined her painting, scrunching her nose critically. "And I want to see them all. And then paint them."

"I'll stay here and keep your studio safe for when you want to come back home."

"Good." Bean twirled to face me, the escaped hair from her bun soft across her face, and smiled. "It'll be nice to come back home to you every once in a while."

"It's always nice to come back home," I said, plumping the pillow and tucking it behind my head.

FALL

I KEEP MY HEAD down, my pen constantly taking notes, even when no one's talking. My feet always move quickly down the hallways, around corners. I breathe normally only when I can hide out in the bathroom during lunch. My locker door has become the new favorite place to stick old, chewed gum. I carry paper towels with me to wipe it off the handle before opening the locker.

The tiny notes tucked in my locker say, *I hate you!!!*

They say, *Fuck u Kayla.*

Killer Kayla doesn't ever seem to get old for them.

By Wednesday, I have mastered the art of tunnel vision, keeping my glassy gaze focused directly in front of me and blurring out everything around me. I don't feel it when they flick my shoulder or when their tobacco-laced spit lands beside my foot. I don't look up when they ask how it feels to be a murderer or even when my teachers call on me to finish a math problem or read out loud in English class.

But I notice when I open my locker and another folded note falls out. My palm automatically shoots forward to catch it. I bite back a sigh. I should throw it away. Instead, I unfold it, like I did with every other note. It's typed. A lot of them are, because anonymity allows for cruelty.

You killed him on purpose.

My nostrils flare and my shoulders shudder through my exhale.

No.

A series of possible reactions sweeps through my mind.

I could drop the note like it's garbage.

Tuck it back in my locker and pretend it doesn't affect me.

Freak the fuck out.

I know I can't look up, around, down the hallway, because the prickling on the back of my neck tells me whoever left this for me could be watching.

Bean?

Jay?

No one can know what I know. What I'm hiding . . . how I'm pretending. And even if someone did know, what would they have to gain by teasing it out of me? This is not a secret Jay wants out in the open. Unless it's a warning: If I stay quiet, he'll stay quiet.

There's a thin sheen of sweat in my hand from holding the note too tight and too long. It takes every last thread of control I can muster to cock my head like I don't understand, shrug, and paste on a smile, and to widen my eyes innocently as I turn around. I don't look for the person who left the note, but close my locker with a snap and drop the note in the nearest trash can, my shaking hand rattling the can too loudly.

"Are you okay?"

Bean is at my side, clutching a pile of books to her chest. Her mouth twists with worry. Bean is always one to worry about everyone else. The nicest girl anyone has ever known.

I take a breath. Clear my throat. Clear every thought out of my head. I don't want to look at her suspiciously. I don't want her to look at me curiously. Waiting for a reaction. I want to pretend the note never existed. "Fine. Why?"

"You look a little . . ." One hand reaches toward my face. I beat her to it, pressing my hand to my cheek. It's cold.

"I'm okay." I drop my hand.

The back-to-school poster on the wall behind Bean catches my attention. The official homecoming game is still weeks away, but other school pride activities begin soon. My glance lands on the kickoff event, the powder-puff game this Saturday. "I was making sure I knew what time the powder-puff game starts on Saturday," I say evenly.

Bean furrows her brow, then turns and reads the poster. Her pale eyebrows rise. "You're going? Do you . . . think that's a good idea?"

I stare at her fingertips clutching the edges of her books so hard that they're white. As though she can see, feel, the way my stomach twists when I think about going to the game. I bite the inside of my mouth to keep the tears from escaping.

A year ago, when we were juniors, the four us had sat in the stands at the annual powder-puff game and cheered on Bean's sister's team.

"Hailey got all the athleticism in the family." Bean had sighed as her sister scored her second touchdown of the first quarter. Jay Brewster, on the sidelines during the plays, ran out each time to lift his girlfriend in the air and swing her around, as though he couldn't bear not being part of it. Even though he'd have his own, much bigger moment in about a month.

"Next year you can be our personal cheerleader," Jen had said to Bean, throwing her arm around my shoulders. "Me and Kayla are going to kick some powder ass."

Competition is a Brewster family trademark. I couldn't imagine having to pit myself against Jay for attention—from this town, from my parents. I'd returned the one-armed hug, pumped my fist high in the air, and let out a whoop. "We'll bury them!"

"You guys are dorks." Selena had laughed as she waved her pom-poms in the air next to us.

"Don't worry, we'll leave some glory for you," Jen had said, wiggling her eyebrows. "College boys like their girls dirty."

"And we all know Selena hates high school boys." I laughed.

"They're slobs!" Selena yelled in the direction of the game.

A couple of guys in the stands below us turned around to see who was shouting, and Selena stuck her tongue out at them.

"Poor, poor high school boys." Bean shook her head.

"Poor high school girls who don't end up on *our* team next year, you mean. We'll destroy them!" Jen yelled. She growled and I growled louder, and eventually we dissolved into laughter.

The girls on the homecoming court always flip a coin before the powder-puff game to determine who will be captains for the two teams. Last year, Jen and I had both expected to be a part of the court, but we'd agreed: if we both ended up as captains senior year, Jen would step down and let another girl take over the second team. And I would pick her for my team first.

Both of us being team captains isn't an issue anymore. Now, it would be a miracle if anyone picks me for their team at all.

And I doubt Bean will be cheering for either me or Jen.

I look away from the poster and back at Bean. Her mouth is soft with sympathy. I can't be near it. *Her.* The way she worries about me and the way I'm not entirely sure if I have or have not failed her.

The way I'm lying to myself. The way I haven't done

enough. The way I want her to say that killing a boy *is* enough. The sacrifices I'm willing for her to make so I can come home again.

The guilt. The guilt that *isn't big enough.*

"Yeah," I tell her as I push back into the river of students moving between classes. Running. Desperately. "It's a good idea."

The smell of smoked and cured pig belly fills the house Saturday morning. The sizzling sound stays near me, relegated to the space where fat pops and burns tiny dots on my arms as I turn the pieces over. I prefer the pain to thinking about what's going to happen in a few hours at the powder-puff game.

"That smells good," Dad says, joining me at the stove. He stares down into the pan with a hopeful expression on his face. "Cooking for a crowd?"

"Not exactly."

"That's a pretty big snack."

He's a terrible hinter.

"I'm hungry. I need energy for the game tonight."

He doesn't seem to notice the way my voice falls flat, instinctively defensive. I don't want him to ask about the game, about my reasons for going. About my first interactions with Jen and Bean and everyone else. He'll want to hear about how everything is fine. That my friends are standing beside me. And when I can't confirm those things, he'll worry about what they're saying. What they might do to me at the powder-puff game. He'll want to protect me.

But I want to protect *him*. He doesn't need to spend his worry on me when he's busy running a farm, especially since it's the first harvest season without Caleb here to help.

I fling a piece of bacon in the pan and the melted fat hits me in the face.

"How was being back at school this week?" he asks as he hands me a paper towel.

I wipe my cheek slowly, watching the bacon finish browning. The question is inevitable, I realize. "Okay."

"People aren't being . . . ?"

"It's fine." The anonymous note left in my locker was the only one that directly referred to what happened that night, except for the ones calling me a killer. And there was no follow-up. I don't know if the occasional knots that tie in my stomach are because I'm not sure who left it for me—and what they want me to do about it—or due to the powder-puff game tonight.

He nods slowly and maybe he believes me when I say it's fine, maybe he doesn't. Either way, he lets it go and I'm grateful. "Right. You need a ride to the game tonight?"

"I'll ride my bike," I say, dishing the bacon strips onto a paper towel–lined plate. "Thanks anyway."

"Enjoy your snack." He snags two pieces, tossing the hot

bacon slices between his hands to cool them, and steps out through the back door.

I watch his long, sure strides until he disappears before I sit down at the kitchen table with my plate.

I can still hear Dad's flat tone as he told me that they were sending me to his sister's in Kansas City. A never-ending echo of disappointment. Now that I'm back, we go about our days like neither of us can remember details: me, what happened that night, and him, that open desperation to get rid of me. It creates a strange tension, the inability to look each other in the eye.

Mom's reaction last May was different. When the alcohol results came in proving that I hadn't been drinking, that it was something else that caused the accident, she only said, "I knew it all along."

There's a certain kind of faith mothers have that makes life bearable.

The crowds are never as big for the powder-puff game as they are for the real homecoming game.

"It's because they call it *powder-puff*," Jen used to say bitterly. "Like we're out on that field with our makeup kits." And then she'd roll her eyes all, *What can we do?*

Still, the south stands, where the late-afternoon sun has warmed the metal, are almost completely full of spectators. The loudest are the alum football players, sneaking sips from flasks hidden down the front of their pants, sexist remarks, as always, at the ready.

"Give me a touchdown, Selena!" someone with a deep voice yells.

"Touch *me* down!" The guy next to him adds, not making much sense but also not seeming to care.

For one of the first times this school year, the abuse isn't for me. Those guys don't care about me and won't, unless my shirt flies up at some point.

Selena folds her arms across her chest and turns her back to the stands, a frown dragging her mouth down.

But the boys still holler. "I like that view better!"

I finish securing my braid. My blood is hot and angry for Selena. For all of us here, just wanting to play the game.

But then the girls on the field notice I've arrived and Selena's eyes light up. She crosses over to me and plants herself close enough that I can smell what she had for dinner.

"Pretty ballsy coming out tonight," she says. Her long, dark hair is held back in a ponytail and with an elastic headband, but a piece has escaped and I can't help watching it as it spills across her high cheekbone.

"I have every right to be here." I dig my palms into my hips, opening my body to her. Proving my fearlessness. She can't see the way I'm pressing my toes into the tops of my shoes to keep steady, though. She can't feel the clenching in my stomach.

In a moment that passes so quickly I wonder if I've imagined it, a flicker of worry draws her eyebrows together. Selena hesitates, searching for the correct next thing to say. We are being watched. She is under pressure.

But she struggles. For one tiny second.

Suddenly she throws her hands against my chest.

I stumble backward, catching myself in a half crouch, as though my life depends on not hitting the ground. My ankle threatens to give way, but I will it to behave. I know I look like an idiot; I hear laughter around me. I feel small and tinny under their comments, and if I could walk away without consequences, I would. But turning my back means they win. It means I'll never be the Kayla I used to be.

"You're going down, bitch." One of their voices sails over to me.

"Careful, that's the killa you're talking to," someone else says.

"Watch out," Selena says in a low voice, just loud enough so I can hear. I can't tell if the warning is malicious or if she's actually concerned.

Across the field, Jen watches us as she adjusts the drawstring in her shorts. Not participating. Not stopping it, either. I am so far away from being able to guess what she's thinking, that it's hard to believe we were best friends.

I step forward again, closer to Selena. "You too."

The homecoming court—Jen and Selena and two girls

who are not me—was voted on the third day of school after a whirlwind campaign of cupcakes, stickers, and empty promises of friendship in exchange for votes. The winners were announced during fifth period the next day. Some people, like Jay and Jen, were shoo-ins from the beginning. I would have been, too, probably. In a different life. But now, the four girls who still belong to this town are called out onto the field, and everyone's attention shifts away from me. I jog slowly in place to warm up as they pick captains. Jen's one of them, holding her yellow flags in two hands.

The rest of us line up along the fifty yard line and wait. I will Jen to look at me. *Remember the promise we made each other last year?*

She doesn't look at me.

But Maria, the other captain, does. And she picks first.

"Kayla Martin," she says without hesitating.

I pretend I get why she picked me first as I sprint over amid hoots and jeers from the field and the stands, take my red flag, and secure it around my waist. My face burns, so I stare at the ground so they can't see. Maybe it's a pity move. Or Maria wants someone she knows can catch a football. Probably, though, she picked me to be a dedicated battering ram.

The teams begin to fill out. Jen picks Selena first. My team huddles before we all take our places on the field. Arms drape over every shoulder but mine.

Mrs. Armstrong, our PE teacher, waits, her silver whistle dangling from her mouth.

"Okay, ladies," Maria says into our small circle of girls, her breathing picking up. "I'm QBing. Hannah, Riley, Fiona, Sarah, and Mel, you're my lineswomen. Patsy, I want you as running back. Kayla, you're going wide. Everyone else . . . just find something useful to do. Let's do this thing."

We clap and emerge from our huddle. Take our positions at the 50-yard line as Hannah is handed the football and drops into a high crouch. We don't do kickoffs in powderpuff. I pick a spot on the far left of our line and look at the player assigned to cover me.

It's Jen.

My mouth goes dry. I press my weight into the balls of my feet and tear my eyes away from the hard challenge on her face.

Mrs. Armstrong blows the whistle and the stands erupt in cheers. My pulse throbs in my neck, rushes through my limbs. Static and words of some sort blare out over the PA system. Sounds are muddied as I trace the route I'll take on the field with my eyes.

"Hike!" Maria yells, and I sprint straight at Jen, fake inside, then blow by on her left-hand side, watching over my shoulder as Maria launches the football in my direction. I'm wide open. I make the catch, tuck the ball under my arm, and face the end zone, just as a pair of hands grabs my ankle.

Pain shoots up my leg and my vision dazzles black and spotty white. I slam, whole-body, into the ground, my breath flying out of me, but hang on to the ball.

Mrs. Armstrong blasts her whistle.

"Sorry, Mrs. Armstrong," Jen says, getting up from her dive. "I was aiming for the flag. Just missed."

"Are you okay, Kayla?" Mrs. Armstrong asks me.

I stand and brush myself off, moving my ankle in a slow circle until I'm sure I can put my weight on it without limping. A few yards away, Maria watches me, a hard line formed by her mouth, and I get it. She picked me because she knows I'll do whatever it takes to win. To belong again.

I nod and suck in a quick breath between my teeth. "I'm fine."

"Kayla Martin with a gain of eighteen yards." A voice comes over the PA system. "First down at the thirty-two."

I wipe my hands on my shorts and take my place on my team's side of scrimmage again. The grass is thick but trimmed short. I stare at it until I catch my breath, then I raise my gaze and lock eyes with Jen.

Bring it.

The afternoon marches on in a blurring series of plays that leave Jen and me both on the ground. Mrs. Armstrong's whistle hardly takes a rest. The spectators have caught on to something happening and the loudest cheers come when Jen or I have added another injury to our bodies. A bruise in her ribs from my elbow. A scrape across my chin from a well-timed trip that sends me flying across the grass.

But neither of us asks for a truce. We're settling a score and I'm hell-bent on coming out on top.

My team is behind by one touchdown at the eight yard line with four minutes to go in the last quarter, and I'm ready to tie it up. Maria's been running the ball the last few plays, but as we huddle, she says, "Get open, Kayla. And don't you *dare* drop the ball."

"No problem."

I line up across from Jen. She looks tired. Her knees are an angry shade of pink. Raw. I've stopped feeling pain—anything—in my bad ankle.

"Hike!"

I dash by the girls battling at the line of scrimmage, then shoot across them on the diagonal, throwing everything I have into this burst of speed. I see Maria pull her arm back and ready myself for the pass. As the ball soars through the air, someone tugs on my braid. My head snaps backward. I spin, keeping my feet under my body, my hands still clamoring for the football. The flash of Jen's ponytail whipping toward me hides her fist.

Five hard knuckles connect with my cheek with a cracking sound. Finally, I go down. The football lands harmlessly in the end zone and rolls away.

Mrs. Armstrong's whistle goes ballistic. My teammates

yell and gesture angrily. The crowd is wild, stomping in the stands. My face throbs. Blood trickles from my nose to my mouth. I wipe it away with the back of my hand.

"What is going on here?" Mrs. Armstrong yells, running over.

Jen holds her arm out to me. Her brown eyes are hard but a little glassy, too. I'm not the only one smarting. "This field is really slick."

I clasp my fingers around her wrist and she hauls me to my feet.

"We keep slipping," I agree breathlessly. Because that's the way things are done. I accept this beating, and it's proof of my dedication to her. To her brother. To this town.

"You have to go off the field until the bleeding stops," Mrs. Armstrong instructs me. I can tell she wants to say something else, but before she can, the crowd's noise rises to a height we haven't heard yet.

We all look to the sidelines. Jay Brewster strides onto the field, followed by half the football team's starting lineup. He's giving everyone his signature *aw-shucks* grin, running a hand through his blond hair, tossing a football casually up and down. People start descending out of the stands to crowd around and cheer on the football heroes. The guys give each other friendly punches in the shoulders, clasp fists, and chest-bump. They start to spread out across the field. And even though we have the field until seven, we know they're here to claim their territory.

Jen and I are the first to look away from the boys. Our expressions, I know, are mirror images of annoyance.

The story of Jen's life.

But Jen recovers in the blink of an eye.

"I guess game's over," she announces with a forced laugh. "We win!"

Her team jumps into a big shrieking pile while the rest of us stand around, wishing this was a more fair game. Maria and the rest of my team are all pissed but not at me, at least. They don't say anything to me. While they plan to go for after-game pizza, I walk back to my bike to head home.

But the bike isn't where I left it.

A girl about six or seven years old playing on the ground notices I'm looking for something and points to the Dumpsters before going back to her dirt castle. My rear tire sticks out the top of the huge metal bin. I sigh.

"I don't know why you played." Noah Michaelson comes up behind me, holding out an old T-shirt.

I take it and wipe my face slowly. I don't owe him an explanation.

He shrugs. "I'll help you get your bike out. Actually . . . want a ride home?"

I drop his shirt back in his outstretched hand and nod.

SPRING

MY EGG SALAD SANDWICH had fallen apart in my backpack before I made it to our table in the cafeteria on Monday.

Jen squeezed her eyes together and stuck her tongue out as I peeled the plastic baggie from its squished contents with a frown. "If you ate normal sandwiches," she said, "you wouldn't have that problem."

I watched her nonchalantly until she took a huge bite of her peanut butter and jelly, then said, "Sorry, what? Didn't hear you."

"I thaid . . ." Her tongue caught on the glob of bread stuck to the roof of her mouth and she grabbed her water bottle, washing her food down in between laughs. "You suck."

"You love me." My shoulders shaking, I got up to grab a spork.

As I searched for a utensil near the bottom of the pile, a finger tapped me on the shoulder.

"Hey, Kayla." Steven McInnis looked over my head instead of at me. He could do that. He was the tallest boy in the school. The thickest, too, probably. The best offensive lineman on the football team. He protected Jay from everything. "You have Olson for physics, right?"

"Yeah."

He pulled an orange plastic lunch tray from the middle of the stack, knocking the top two on the floor. As he bent to pick them up, he said, "I know this is last-minute, but do you think I could get your help with the test this week?"

"I'm not taking it." I grabbed a small pile of napkins from the dispenser. Steven's eyes flickered back and forth and his fingers drummed on the tray. "I have an A so I get to drop the last test. A policy that made Olson my new favorite teacher this year."

"Yeah, she's cool. But I have to take it." He moved into the lunch line, herding me along with him.

I glanced over at my table. Selena was telling a story and using big hand gestures. Her hand gesture stories were always good. I was getting impatient.

But Steven pushed on. "Do you still think you could help me pass this test? Please? You have an A and I have to pass it to—"

"Dude." Jay Brewster caught up with us. Steven adjusted his angle so I could slip out from between him and the lunch counter as Jay slapped Steven's shoulder. "We have already been over this. No one's going to fail you. I'll make sure of it."

Steven stared at the cafeteria worker as she piled noodles on his plate, paused to glance up at him, then piled some more. "I know, man, but like I said before, I actually want to learn this stuff."

"You had all semester to learn it," Jay said. "Should have done it then. I don't need my guys coming up for ineligibility."

"I should have." Steven slammed his plate on his tray and scooted down to grab two chocolate milks. "But I didn't. I have to get a ninety-five on this test just to pass the class. Kayla said she'll help me out with it."

"Um, what? No, I didn't. I don't have time for that." The spork in my hand snapped. I frowned and moved away to grab another one.

But Jay's voice rose above the din in the cafeteria. "Neither do you, man. Spring training after school all week. Can't risk missing it. There's something like six guys who want your spot. I told you. I'll take care of it."

I didn't want to know how Jay was going to take care of Steven's failing physics grade, and really, I didn't care. Even with the way Steven was giving me helpless eyes while Jay fussed with the bags of chips, looking for his favorite.

New spork in hand, I went back to my table and poked at my egg salad mash.

"Steven's failing physics," I said between mouthfuls. "Wants me to tutor him for the test this week. Do we know anyone who would actually do that?"

"No," Selena immediately said. "People have lives." She

brushed her ponytail over her shoulder and speared a piece of lettuce. "I hate salads."

"Then don't eat them," Jen said.

"Maria is on the warpath about the cheer uniforms for next year. She wants to go back to pleats. And this ass? Is not flattered by pleats."

"You look great in *everything*," Bean cut in. Then she said to me, "I would help Steven out if I was taking physics. Maybe Leo Marshall?"

I shrugged. "Maybe. I'll mention Leo next time I see Steven, but I'm not hunting someone down for him. Like Jay said, he had all year to pass this class."

Jen's stack of bangles jangled when she raised her arm to eat her yogurt. The weather was warm enough for bare shoulders, if only the school dress code allowed it. We both wore cap sleeves. As close to tank tops as we could get and still slide by the rules.

"What else did Jay say?" she said.

"He said he'd take care of it."

"Jesus." She slammed her spoon on the table and someone down the line jumped. "Seriously? He really thinks he can get Steven out of this just by being Jay fucking Brewster? He just has no concept of reality. I can't even."

"Calm down," Selena said, raising her eyebrows at Jen's sudden outburst. "It's just talk."

"Yup. Steven knows it. That's why he's looking for a

tutor." I nudged Jen's shoulder with mine and she gave me a halfhearted smile. Most of the time, even she realized when she overreacted to her brother. But he did get away with a lot more than she did. I'd be frustrated, too, if I were her. "Anyway, I think you'll look cute in pleats, Selena. Don't worry about it."

Selena tossed her fork into the plastic salad container and stood. "Good. Because nothing is worth eating this crap."

Bean shook her head as Selena took her lunch to the garbage bins. "I like vegetables."

"Do vegetables silently cry when you pick them?" Jen teased.

Bean was the only vegetarian we knew. Also the only one who came from a family that raised their own cows for meat. I knew those things were linked. *They're so cute*, she'd tell us about her family's shaggy Highland cows. *Their big eyes and floppy hair. I just can't eat them.*

"Ha-ha," Bean said.

Steven slid into an empty seat next to Bean from his end of the table. Most people towered over Bean, but Steven and his long chunky limbs did especially.

"About helping with my test, Kayla," he began, but I cut him off.

"Have you asked Leo Marshall?"

"He said no. I think he's still mad about the bus incident."

"You mean the way you harassed him on the bus all last year? I remember some name you called him . . . Marshall Mincemeat?"

Steven snorted and rubbed his neck. "Yeah. Okay, whatever. T. J. came up with that one. That's his thing. *And* it's history. We've moved on."

"Sounds like *he* hasn't."

Steven closed his eyes and took a calming breath. "Kayla, come on. Help me out, please. I'm begging you."

I gathered the remnants of my lunch and stuffed them back in my paper bag. "I don't really have time for that. I have chores and riding practice all week, then helping Jen get ready for her party."

"You're coming, right?" Jen said.

"If I'm not grounded forever," Steven said. He pressed his palms against the table for a second. His letter jacket hung on his shoulders like he'd actually lost weight over the winter. I knew he had started working after school to help out at home after his mom went on disability. I didn't know how he was going to juggle a job plus football this year. A pang of guilt squeezed my chest. He really wanted to pass this class.

I sighed. "Look, I can't do anything until Wednesday, but if you can come over and help me finish my chores, I'll help you with the test."

His one crooked tooth pressed on the side of his lip when

he grinned. He pushed himself to his feet with a little hop. "I will get you through those chores faster than lightning. And I'll totally study as much as I can before then. You have saved my life, Kayla. I owe you."

"I'll just give you the grossest chores," I said to his retreating back.

"That was nice," Bean said, looking at me with a small smile on her face.

"*Too* nice." Selena towered over the table, her hands on her hips. "Like you said, he had his chance already. But whatever. I have to run to a cheer meeting. Someone has to try to vote down the pleats."

"I'll walk with you." Bean flung her leg over the bench. "Ms. Norris is giving feedback on our portfolios if we go in during lunch."

"Me too," Jen said, slurping the last of her yogurt. "I found those library books I checked out at the beginning of the year. Nice timing, right? I can check more out just in time for the year to be over. Coming, Kayla?"

I shook my head. "I'm sitting my butt right here for the next twenty minutes, then out on the lawn after because I have free period next. Getting As in physics, after all." I couldn't hide my smug smile.

"Lazy," Selena said.

"Jealous," I retorted.

My three best friends laughed as they wove around

cafeteria tables and into the school halls. I pulled out a book and tried to concentrate. After reading the same paragraph five times in a row, I realized the only voice in my head belonged to Jay Brewster.

I'll take care of it.

FALL

WE TOSS MY BIKE in the back of Noah's truck.

"Nice game, anyway," he says as I fumble for a tissue in his glove compartment to shove up my still-bleeding nose.

"Thanks."

My muscles are tight. I am bruised all over. A sickening feeling weighs me down. I trace a crack in his dash with one finger.

Noah clears his throat and sneaks a glance at me. "Why did you go to that game?"

"It's a free country," I tell him, searching the horizon beyond the playing fields. I'm not sure what I'm looking for, only that I can tell he hasn't moved his warm brown eyes from me and I don't want to look at him. I don't know why he's being so nice to me.

"That's not what I meant." Noah starts the truck and pulls out of the parking lot. We're quiet, and I know that even though he isn't looking at me anymore, he's waiting for some other explanation from me. He turns the steering wheel, aiming the tires for a pothole in the road so that we both jump in our seats and bonk the top of the cab with our heads. I want to laugh at his childish driving maneuver, but it feels strangely vulnerable to laugh with him. To share that kind of intimacy.

Humor. To let him pull out a piece of the old, happy Kayla when so much about who I am now . . . aches.

"Yeah," I say, finally, with a sigh. I know what his question means. But I can't tell him that game was all the reasons I did what I did and all the reasons I came back. He wouldn't understand. Noah Michaelson has never been on the inside like I was. Never seemed to care about sports or spirit week or parties spilling across the banks of the river.

I rub my head and look out the window into a dark, fallow field, imagining the listless brown soil bursting with baby green life. The promise of early springtime. Change and renewal.

I push my long bangs out of my face, wondering if the dark shadows under my eyes hide the greens and yellows of my hazel eyes, and focus on the view out the window, judging how far I can see before a tall building mars the landscape. Here, in a patch between barns and houses, I can see a long ways away, the first flickering of light seemingly as far as the moon.

We drive in silence another mile. The dust flies behind the tires of the truck, creating a cloud that rises, billows out behind us. Noah pulls off onto another dirt road. The dirt roads out here crisscross forever like the lines over the top of a ball of yarn.

"I live on Sunview," I tell Noah.

He hesitates before answering and I realize he already

knows that. Because I know where he lives, too. We all know where everyone lives in a town like this. But my memory tickles with something more. Playing together as children, a long time ago. The scent of food no one in this town but his mom cooks. He doesn't mention a long-forgotten history. He says only, "Oh. Okay."

When we get close, I point out my house. Unnecessarily but for some reason I need this control. This pretending Noah isn't as much a part of this town's landscape as he is. His otherness draws me to him, to the idea that he won't—can't—hate me as much as everyone else. Because he is not like them? Or because he is like me? I don't know which. None of the above.

Maybe he's just a good person and that's it.

His hand on the steering wheel is sure as he slips into my driveway. I glimpse a movement in the front window. Ella, my family hound dog, watches us, her dark eyes flickering with interest. When we take too long to get out of the truck, she howls forlornly. My fingers tap the edge of the door handle silently, manically, a sporadic rhythm.

"Okay. We're here," he says after a moment. Then: "You smell like bacon. Dirty, sweaty bacon."

I laugh like I haven't for a long time.

My laughter opens a space between us that he fills with his smile. It's a great smile, lighting up his face, reaching to the corners of his eyes. His shoulders relax. "I remember you always being on a horse. You used to ride by my house a lot. Did you ride in Kansas City?" he asks.

Those were quiet days, when Jen and I ambled for hours down the roads and trails that led past his house, only a mile or so from mine. I can picture the yellow siding and white trim. His mom gardening in the front yard, wearing a wide-brimmed straw hat. A small woman. Skin the same color as Noah's, but dark hair to go with it.

The time I really knew him feels so long ago. But I can almost see the inside of his house. The cross on the wall. The thick rugs under bare feet. I don't recall him being around at all much the last several years, as though he'd slipped into some quiet shadow place. As though people like me and my old friends put him there.

I look at him again, surprised but grateful to see kindness in his eyes. "No. I don't ride anymore. I've lost interest."

"Oh. I thought that was your thing."

It used to be my *favorite* thing. I loved the way the air combed my hair like invisible fingers when Caramel Star and I sprinted across the back fields and the way I seemed to grow wings as we jumped fences in gravity-defying weight-lessness. The beautiful ache in my ab and thigh muscles. The coming down, catching our breath, as I slowly brushed her flanks after.

But now, my injured ankle spasms even as I just think about riding.

My heart bursts because my horse is boarded at Jen's.

"You know how they put down racing horses when they break their ankles?"

"You're not the horse, though," he says. "You're the rider."

My back stiffens. "It's not that easy."

"Sure it is. Like riding a bike, right? Just get up there and—"

"*I can't do it anymore.*"

Silence fills the cab of the truck. I check my tone. Open the door. Say, meekly, "Thanks for the ride, Noah."

I catch his "No problem" just before the door slams closed behind me.

SPRING

MY PRIMARY REASONS FOR showing up at school that last Wednesday of classes were to turn in my last paper for English class and to get my yearbook signed. Jen and Selena and Bean and I crammed our heads together over the yearbook at lunch, first checking our class photos—we laughed at how Bean wasn't looking at the camera but at some point over the top of it—and then flipping through to count how many other club and social photos we were in.

Selena was all over the cheerleaders' page, while Jen and I were part of a special spread on "Horsemanship at Ulysses S. Grant High."

"Thank you, Noah Michaelson," Jen said.

The photo of Bean receiving her county art award for a pastel piece she'd done of the landscape viewed from Point Fellows in the fall was taken at profile.

"Bean," I said, "are you one of those people who believes looking directly at the camera steals your soul?"

"Maybe. That would explain a lot about the three of you." She hooked her hands into the big square pockets at the front of her circle skirt. Pulled out a half-empty tube of white acrylic paint, looked at it, puzzled, and replaced it in her pocket with a shrug.

"Well, I don't believe in souls at all," Selena said.

T. J. crossed the lunchroom and sat next to me, catching the end of Selena's statement. "Why not?" he said.

"Because it's inconvenient. My Catholic soul is destined to burn in hell if I do anything wrong. It's not worth the anxiety to believe when it's so much more freeing *not* to. If I went to confession, the priest would die of shock."

"I doubt that," T. J. scoffed.

"Just tell her you agree." Jen turned the page in the yearbook and squinted at the members of the French club. "She has a reputation to uphold."

I pulled the yearbook out of Jen's hands and flipped to the back pages where the candid photos were. In the center of one page, a large photo of the four of us was framed by black swirls. It was taken at last fall's homecoming carnival. Jen and I stood on the left and Selena and Bean on the right, but all four of us were held tightly together by arms around one another's shoulders. Selena wore her cheer uniform. Bean wore a lacy, cream-colored dress, and Jen wore shorts and a flowery, button-up top over a T-shirt. I had on jeans slung low across my hips and a tank top. Each one of us was wearing a big grin. Even Bean was looking at the camera in this one. Behind us, the setting sun haloed our heads in a flare of reddish-yellow color.

Looking at the photo raised sacred memories: the scents of fried foods and hay and the feeling of a breeze growing cooler as evening came. That was the night Caleb went six rounds at the dunk tank, sending Tory Worth into the water over and over again because he was too intimidated by her to just ask her out. She hated him from that day on.

"This is my favorite picture," I said, laying the book flat on the table and pressing my hands over the page. "I might have slipped it to Noah along with our riding photos."

"I love that," Jen said softly.

"Noah . . . Michaelson? He goes to my church," Selena said. "Weird guy. Quiet."

"You say that every time I mention his name." I squinted at her. "I thought you didn't believe in church."

"Don't believe in souls," she corrected. She shrugged. "But church . . . it's a *thing*. Being Catholic in a town like this, you all stick together because of *community* or something like that." She nosed in close to see the photo, then sat back with a smug smile and nudged Bean's shoulder. "And on that topic, there goes our theory about your soul. I guess you just can't be bothered to look at the camera most of the time."

Bean shrugged and smiled at us.

Behind her, Jay and Steven and the rest of the guys who sat on the other side of our table were getting to their feet. I shouted, "Hey, Steven, what time are you coming by?"

Steven shoved a last handful of limp fries in his mouth and shook his head. His food was only half chewed when he opened his mouth to answer me. "Oh yeah. Don't worry about it. I got this." He tipped the rest of his milk into his mouth, swished it around his cheeks, and swallowed.

"Did you find someone else to help?" I asked.

"Something like that. Got to run, though. See ya." He swept his tray off the table, dropping and ignoring half his food that had fallen on the floor, and followed Jay out of the cafeteria. I made a face at his retreating back.

"Jerk. I left mucking out mom's chicken coop till today because I thought he was coming over."

"They're all jerks," Jen said breezily. She closed the yearbook and handed it back to me, her dimple deep in her cheek. "Anyway, I love that picture of us. We look hot."

I stashed the yearbook in my backpack and zipped it. "Speaking of physics, I haven't decided which science I'm taking next year. I should take health sciences because it's more nurse-y, but that forensic sciences class Olson started last fall sounds so fun."

"I want to take the forensic class, too," Jen said. "But I should probably go with AP bio. I want to get as many college courses out of my way as possible, and unless there's a new AP forensics, it's not going to happen for me."

I wrinkled my nose. "Harvey teaches AP bio. That's rough." Mr. Harvey was older than the earth and yelled because he couldn't hear himself speaking.

"Harvey teaches all the AP science classes," Jen corrected. "And yeah, it sucks. I would want Olson, too."

We finished lunch under a steadily growing roar of sound, as we had all week. Students were restless during the last few days of school. I drilled the girls on our summer plans yet again. Selena had to go to cheer camp in August, but before that, planned to work all summer. Bean was visiting her aunt in California for a month. As for me and Jen, we had plans to travel to six states for riding competitions and then we were joining her parents for a cruise to the Bahamas.

"I know it's *ages* away," Jen said, "but we can look at swimsuits tomorrow when we go shopping for outfits for the party."

"Sounds good." I gathered my things, draping my backpack over my shoulder. "I have to run. I'm going to see if I can get in with my counselor before the lunch bell rings and ask for her opinion on next year's science."

The hallways were jammed with groups of people signing yearbooks. A few senior guys high-fived over something— probably a yearbook quote they thought was particularly funny. Three girls smiled at their photos as tears streamed down their faces. Hailey Patterson and her best friend, Ingrid, pointed at a spot on a page. Ingrid tipped her head to the side with a little smile, but Hailey frowned. Hailey looked up to see me staring and I looked away quickly. I wondered if what made her eyes narrow like that was the photo of her and Jay at last fall's powder-puff game, him raising her into the air in a victory move. I had done a double take when

I saw that photo for the first time, too.

I shouldered my way to the main office and checked my guidance counselor's sign-up sheet. She was booked for the next two hours, but I knew I could get a late slip from her for sixth period, so I picked up the pencil to add my name to the list. I'd written the first K when a loud "What!" made me look up.

Behind the secretaries' desks, four figures shadowed the frosted glass windows into the principal's office. Voices were raised inside, although now that I was paying closer attention, I could also make out another voice hissing at everyone to quiet down. For a moment, I thought someone would tell me to hurry up with my sign-up and get on my way, but the office secretaries' fingers were paused over phones and computer keyboards. Everyone wanted to hear what was being said.

". . . cannot make that call . . . am the teacher?" It was a woman's voice.

"New . . . understand . . ." came Principal Brady's voice.

"Your incomplete syllabus . . . can't penalize a student . . . having responsibilities."

"That syllabus was approved by *you*, Chuck," the female said over the other voices, referring to Principal Brady. "And this has nothing to do with football! He's *failing!*"

The principal's door opened. I dropped my head quickly, taking a full minute to write the "a" on the end of my name.

"Steven has one more chance to pass, is that right, Ms. Olson?"

"He has to pass tomorrow's test with a ninety-five," she said. Only her hand and the tip of her red pump were visible around the frame of the door. Principal Brady still hadn't looked up into the main office.

"Let me know when he does that," a slick voice said. Coach Hillyer.

"If he does, I will be more than happy to," Ms. Olson said. "I want my students to succeed."

"Look," the coach said. "I'm on your side. I don't want to fight. If he doesn't pass, I'll make him do some work around the locker rooms. We'll call it anatomy, you can give him extra credit for it, and it'll be sorted out."

Finally, Ms. Olson came into full view. Her mouth was set in a thin line and her eyes blazed with anger. "I'm not passing him just because you tell me to. Anatomy has *nothing* to do with physics. Nor do you have any say in whether or not my students get extra credit. I have principles. I'll leave this school before I let you push me around." She brushed by Principal Brady and slammed through the swing door past the secretaries' desks. She didn't look at me when she passed.

In the principal's office, the coach made some laughing comment about having all summer to find a replacement. Vice Principal Green slipped out between them, rubbing the deep wrinkles in his forehead between his thumb and fore-finger.

I looked down at my name on the sign-up sheet. I'd written it so slowly that the markings were thick and dark. With a sigh, I flipped the pencil over and erased my name. There would be no fun forensic science for anyone. Because I knew how it worked around here, even if Ms. Olson didn't. Unless she passed Steven, she and her principles weren't going to be back next year.

In the hallway, Jay Brewster lounged against a water fountain, waiting for Steven to finish his drink. He looked up at me and grinned.

"Hey, Kayla, I think you're off the hook for tutoring Steven. He's going to be doing some extra-credit stuff with Coach."

Steven stood upright and wiped the back of his hand slowly across his mouth. When his eyes caught mine, I saw some mix of hard resilience and shame in them. Or maybe that was just my imagination. Maybe all that was really there was triumph. Or even nothing at all. It was just the way of things.

"Too bad," I said. "I was saving cleaning my mom's chicken coop for you. Now I have to clean it myself." I poked out my bottom lip.

Jay pushed off with his hip and crossed the hall. Someone had drawn hearts and flowers and peace signs on the back of his left hand with a blue pen. A girl with a crush on him, probably. His abashed grin showed off his straight, white teeth.

"Sorry about that. Know what? We'll do it anyway. Won't we, Steve?" Jay nodded over his shoulder. "Coop's on the side of the house, right? Just leave the supplies out for us and we'll come after practice and get it cleaner than it's ever been. It's the least we can do since you were so cool about tutoring, right, man?"

"Absolutely." Steven stuffed his hands in his jeans pockets and nodded.

I wanted to feel irritated. Most of the time, the football program's weight tossing around here didn't affect me. But I also really didn't want to muck out the coop.

As Jay snaked his arm across my shoulders and nodded at a couple of cheerleaders passing by, I debated. Did I want to make a point, say something that would piss Jay off, or did I want to let it go, knowing anything I said wouldn't matter anyway? I reached into my bag and fidgeted with the edge of a notebook. At least he'd offered to clean the coop.

I blew out a huff of air. "I'll leave the cleaning stuff out for you. I expect it to be sparkling, though."

"You're a cool girl, Kayla. We'll dedicate next season to you or something." Jay squeezed my shoulders.

I made a dismissive noise and went off to hang out on the hill.

FALL

I FLIP OVER ONTO my stomach, drop my arm down so that my fingers graze the floor, and look around my bedroom. It's a mess and I still haven't gotten out of bed, even though Dad's been in the field for hours by now.

Mom made breakfast. I know because I could smell it, because I heard her when she came upstairs and opened my door, prepared to invite me down. I wasn't sleeping. I just pretended to be.

Without riding practice, my weekends are wide open. At my aunt's, I'd head to the park a few blocks from her house and lie on the grass for hours. Or I'd go downtown and explore, trying to make a map of the city in my head. Anything to take up mind-space. Here, though, after chores, there's little else to do. But that doesn't mean I want to stay in bed all day. My toes wiggle on the cold wood floor as I get up and get dressed.

Downstairs, Mom is organizing jam in the pantry. I open the dishwasher and start to unload clean dishes.

"What does Dad want me to do today?" I say to Mom's back.

She pulls her head out of the pantry to peek at me. "Thanks for unloading that. But I don't think he's expecting you out there today. You should take a couple of weeks off. Settle back in. Your Aunt Bea called this morning and I told her you're taking it easy. Don't want to make a liar out of me, do you?"

I think about the third text Bea had sent last night, after Noah Michaelson dropped me off. She asked me to call her to check in. "What else did you tell her?"

I hear a canister of something small—beans or rice— shift. "I told her your nightmares don't seem to be giving you trouble." Another canister slides across a shelf. I never talked to my parents about the nightmares, so Aunt Bea must have told them. I can imagine the exact tone Mom's voice would have had in that conversation. The calm acceptance that almost conceals her concern. She probably brought up the possibility of therapy again, even though I refused to go twice already. Now, Mom doesn't press. She leaves her statement as fact and moves on. "Do you have homework this weekend?"

"Some. Not a lot." I carefully stack plates on the shelf above me. "I could move bales of hay—"

"No." Mom turns away from her organizing and closes the pantry door. "Just relax, Kayla."

"Right." I finish unloading the dishwasher, pull a soda from the garage fridge, and head out back to the boat. It's exactly as I left it months ago. The boards replaced and waiting for sanding. It's not the only thing waiting outside.

"What are you doing here?" I ask Noah Michaelson, who is standing beside my boat. There's a line of sweat rolling down his temple and he lifts the bottom of his T-shirt to wipe it away. I stare, unabashed, at the narrow line running down his abdomen until he drops his shirt again, a tinge of red building across his cheekbones.

"Helping your dad move hay. Have to really start saving this year for college. Just finished, actually. Saw the boat on my way out. Cool project."

"I could have helped with the hay. We didn't need you."

Noah raises his dark eyebrows and I shrug.

"Sorry for being rude."

"Sorry and a Coke would be nice."

I snort and orange spittle flies from my nose. I wipe my face and say, "The garage fridge. Help yourself."

I sit and pick up the sander, then set it down again when Noah comes back with his Coke.

Instead of turning on the power tool, I climb into the boat and rest my head on the bench. "Have you been in a boat before?"

"Sure." He shrugs. "Lake vacations. Whenever I go to the Philippines. My uncles are fishermen."

"Do you like it? Being on the water?"

"I take pills so I don't get seasick. But otherwise . . . it's fine."

"Oh, I haven't thought about getting seasick. Hm."

"I'm sure you'll be fine." He sips his Coke. Is silent for a moment. Blurts out, "Why'd you come back, Kayla?"

I look up at him, shielding my eyes from the bright sun with my hand. "Should I not have?"

"I don't know." He looks down at his feet. "Should you have? I don't really pay attention to what people say, you know. Call it a defense mechanism after so many years of . . ." He pulls off the tab on his Coke and sticks it in his pocket instead of finishing his sentence. "So, why come back? Why did you leave in the first place?"

"I think everyone knows why I left." I pause. Shouts from the workers in the fields distract me and I have a hard time forming thoughts. "I came back because . . . I'm not entirely sure. Because this is home." I pause. "And I deserve to be here."

"Because you can't let other people drive you away from what's yours," he says.

"Yeah. Something like that."

Noah balances on the edge of the boat. "It was an accident."

"That's what they say. Some of them."

I turn the orange soda can in my palms, bringing it close to my face so I can stall while I read the ingredients label. Nothing to get excited about. Not a single mention of actual fruit.

"Aunt Bea is pretty great," I continue. "She took me in

even though she didn't know what to do with me. She's older than my dad and never had any kids. So, here's this niece coming to stay. To hide. After doing something horrible. But it didn't even faze her. She said it was an accident. That towns like this . . . people here just need time."

"Was it an accident?"

My head whips toward him. I stare for a moment, trying to slow my swirling mind. "Was it an accident?" I whisper.

His face is blank. I try to remember him at Jen's party. When he showed up, who he came with. But there's nothing.

As though he can see into my mind, where I'm sifting through memories of that night, he says, "I left before it happened. Had to take someone home. So I didn't hear what people were saying. Not until later."

What they were saying. The moment they heard a truck had totaled Steven McInnis's car. The moment they heard sirens speed down the road. Even then, Noah's words suggest, they questioned whether it was an accident. I clutch the can until it dents. "The only people who know if it was an accident or not were in the car. Either way, T. J.'s right. I killed someone."

The moment I say it is the moment I want Noah to understand how much I mean it. How much the guilt eats at me. So much guilt. I *killed* someone.

"An accident," he repeats.

Without warning, my eyes begin to sting, my head

begins to ache. I watch him trace his finger along the place two boards meet. In another field, an engine roars to life. A breeze dips in and out of the boat.

Noah looks at me. His face is soft, understanding. Different from my aunt's stern strength, from my dad's hesitant awkwardness, from my mom's steady confidence. It's kind, compassionate, exactly what I need right now.

I struggle not to choke up when I ask, "Do you think people will ever forgive me?" He's silent too long and I sigh. "People here are stubborn."

"I'm not," he tells me. I raise my eyes to his even though I want to hide the tears gathering there. Because I want to see proof of what I thought I heard in his voice. And it's there, in the set of his jaw, in the steadiness of his gaze on me: hope. A force that pushes my feet forward when I'm tired of moving against a current of people who hate me, who don't understand. My hope combined with Noah's makes me feel like I can take on this whole town and everything I've ever done wrong.

He reaches for my hand suddenly and presses the pad of his thumb to mine. When he blinks at me, with the sunlight dying in the distance, his dark lashes make tiny shadows across the tops of his cheeks.

I feel the pressure of his finger on my hand long after the sun has set over Missouri. Before I fall asleep, it's his face in my thoughts that makes me feel like tomorrow can be different. Better. But in the morning, all that remains is a conviction that he is wrong.

My feet drag me through the school hallways, past the stealthy glances and whispers that burrow under my skin. Every time I answer a question in class, Selena shoots me a disgusted look. Even worse, Jen ignores me like I haven't said anything at all.

There are moments when some other minor school scandal or joke takes attention away from me. But it always comes back. The names, the scowls, the low murmurs that surround me as I stand in the entrance to the cafeteria at lunchtime, scanning desperately for an empty table, the smell of egg salad drifting up from my bag and making my stomach roil until I turn away and dart for the bathroom, hacking spittle into the sinks.

Earlier today, the Warrior Squad delivered goody packages to the football players. Eve Karkova brought three into my first period class. One for T. J. and one for Pete Sloan. And then she paused, pursing her lips and looking over at me. I recalled the last time I saw her at Jen's party. Jay and Hailey were broken up by then and Eve had wasted no time swooping in on him. Her flirty, high-pitched laugh rang in my ears as she crossed the room now, frowning, and dropped the last spirit package on my desk. I froze, not knowing what to do with it while classmates' eyes burned into my back. I considered moving it to the windowsill, but my hand felt like stone as I reached for it, for the tag with his name on it, too heavy to lift.

Steven McInnis.

In the end, I leave it on my desk the entire period, my belly muscles clenched and breath held in spurts of one or two minutes at a time until I see black fuzz and stars at the edges of my vision.

When the bell rings, I wait until everyone else has left the room and slip away, relieved, from the reminder of a dead boy. I'm wearing big hoop earrings for '80s Day, the kick-off to Spirit Week. They swing fiercely as something hits me from behind in the hallway, slamming me into my locker. I bite back a cry and spin around. T. J.

His back is to me. A tall, muscular back ending sharply at his shoulders. I remember wanting my hands on those shoulders once.

T. J. turns and faces me slowly, his eyebrows raised. Pretending he hadn't known I was there. The football he's just caught cradled in his hands.

"*Oops.* Toss went a little long, I guess." He slams into my shoulder hard enough to knock my bag on the floor. He almost knocks *me* on the floor. "Oops again. Slipped." He watches me for a second, his full lips twitching with a humorless smile.

I squat to gather the papers that scattered across the floor.

My hair shades my face. It drapes across my shaking shoulders. When I look up, T. J.'s reached the end of the hallway.

Jay Brewster waits there for him. He's watching me. How long has he watched me? I can't help my gaze moving to his arm, the one that was fractured in the crash. It's fine now. Still throws a great long ball. *He's* fine. He didn't die. I didn't die. The crash was only enough for me to get away . . . and months later, an opening just big enough for me to crawl back home. When I look back at his face, his chin juts out under a frown.

He's supposed to see, understand, the pact I've made: I give him my silence and he gives me my life back. *That's how it's supposed to work.*

But it's like he can't see it. Or won't.

My hand pauses on a homework assignment, and my breath comes quickly. I feel like I have a second, one moment to do the perfect thing. Mouth something that will show everyone how sorry I am or make some kind of motion to express how I feel, but I can't think of anything.

And then my mind is taken over by a redness, a rage, a fear. Remembering the last things Jay said to me. Remembering wanting to hurt him . . . more than I had. Wanting to hurt him as much as I hurt Steven.

T. J. tosses Jay the football back, and the steely look Jay gives me is a warning. He spins around, and by the time I've caught my breath again, the moment is gone.

* * *

Noah finds me down the back hallway to the gym. The one
no one uses except to skip class. I spend half a second wondering how I've seen him more in the days I've been back
home than I did in three years of high school before saying,
"I've decided to go to the pancake breakfast."

He clucks his tongue and joins me on the floor. "Why?"

"To talk to Jay."

"That sounds ominous."

"Oh, good word," I say.

He ignores me, fishing around in his backpack for something.

"I just feel like . . . I mean, it's going to take this huge
burst of courage to talk to him, you know? Tell him I'm sorry.
About the accident . . . Steven. But if I do it while I'm showing him support at the same time, maybe it'll go better than
if I went to his house or something."

He brings forth a Twix and lets out a low whistle. "You're
ready to face Jay and *everyone else*? I'm not sure if you're
brave or stupid."

The annual pancake breakfast comes at the end of Spirit
Week and the whole town shows up. The homecoming court
serves the food, raising money for the town's scholarship
fund.

"Probably both. But what's the worst he could do? Refuse
to talk to me?"

"Yeah, that's probably the worst he could do."

"If nothing else, Erica Brewster can't be horrible to me in public."

"If she is, I'll remind her about the time she drove her car into the side of Mackleby's Diner."

"You know about that?"

He gives me a look. "Everyone does."

I bite my lip and look away from him. There's a thick coating of grime where the wall meets the linoleum floor. An empty, crushed water bottle rests within reach. He holds out the open Twix package and I take one of the pieces, letting the chocolate melt over my fingers.

"Your friend Selena was at church on Sunday."

"She doesn't go to church. I mean, she goes, but she doesn't believe in any of it. Doesn't do confession and all that."

"She does. Or . . . she did. One time, at least. I don't know if it's more than that. I was dropping my mom off at church for her weekly coffee social awhile ago and Selena came out of the confessional right when I walked in. I don't think she saw me. I guess she could have just been taking a nap in there or something," he says.

"Why?" I wonder aloud.

"I don't know. I see her, but I don't talk to her."

"You don't really talk to anyone."

"I talk to you."

"Why?"

"Because no one else does."

I squeeze my eyelids shut. Open them and take a bite of candy. "Do you like going to church?"

"Yeah."

"You believe in all of it?" If he notices the flutter in my voice, he doesn't mention it.

"There's a difference between going to church because it's a place I belong and going to church because I believe in it." He shrugs and takes a nibble off the end of his Twix.

I fidget, running a fingernail over my upper arm, scratching a phantom itch. "Don't you believe any of it?"

"I believe enough."

I wait for him to elaborate, but he doesn't. He shifts uncomfortably and I know it's time to talk about something else. It's not like I can give him a hard time for not explaining everything about himself. We both keep some things to ourselves. In another life, that would have bothered me, but now I don't have a leg to stand on.

"How's Steven McInnis's family been holding up after everything?" I say.

"I don't know. What would you expect?"

"I don't know." I blink. My forehead wrinkles. How would I feel if Caleb was killed? "It's probably awful."

Steven had been sitting behind Jay, the worst place possible, when I turned the car into the ditch. When I saw, too late, the truck cresting the hill and I tried to spin away from it. That truck demolished the passenger side of the car, the heaviest impact in the rear. Steven wasn't wearing a seat belt. The doors on my side flew open on collision, throwing both me and Steven from the car. Feet away, a mile away. It didn't matter. The newspaper said he'd died instantly. It was a dead body flung from the car.

Noah must see the blame that weighs down my shoulders because he reaches his hand out to me, letting it drop before his fingers quite reach mine. "It was an accident, Kayla."

"How do you know?"

"It was a dark night on a freshly oiled road, and I don't know, the truck's lights were probably too high. Blinding. What else could it have been?"

The paint is peeling on the ceiling. Fat half curls of it. I count each curl until I lose the temptation to confess everything to Noah. It would feel so good to come clean. But telling him what I know would test this . . . whatever we are right now. Friends? People Who Talk? I don't know who we would be on the other side of my admission. Only that it would probably be bad. My ankle unexpectedly seizes into a spasm of pain and I pull my leg toward my stomach then stretch it out again. I can manage the throb. I can manage this.

"I don't care what they say or think. If they forgive you or not. Do you ever think you don't need it? Forgiveness.

From anyone. That an accident is just that? Something awful that happened. Not anyone's fault." It's a whisper, gentle and inexplicably caring, and I want to enfold myself in the comfort of it.

"It's my fault if people say it is."

I get to my feet and walk to the tall, rectangular windows along the walls, the metal frames weathered and weakened. The school sits on a hill and from here I can look out over this town, this state, a sky that runs from city to village, civilization to wilds, dust to river here.

"I want to be able to go home."

He watches me for a silent moment, his eyes perusing the planes of my face. "You are home."

I spin. Rest my palm on the windowsill. Catch and hold his gaze. "Can I ask you a favor, Noah?"

"Depends on what it is."

"Will you drive me out to the McInnises'?"

"Now?"

I nod. He stands and stuffs his hands in his pockets, watching me for a moment. His jaw works twice. Then he pulls his keys out and motions for me to follow him.

We cross Third Street and keep going. In the distance, the river snakes to the edges of town, an area that's come to be known as the back side. Where we're headed. The houses out here face the industrial parks where grain is stored and the huge freezers where pork is frozen before being loaded on the trains running through, sparingly at some points in the year, twice daily during harvests. Homes look like they've been rattled one too many times by those trains. Paint chips are missing off porches, and roofs are uneven where tiles have gone lost. The houses lean, all in the same direction, as though the wind has pushed at their walls one too many times and they're too tired anymore to fight back and stand upright.

I know Steven McInnis lived out here, but I don't know which house.

"You don't have to do this," Noah says, creeping down a gravel road, navigating potholes.

"I have to do this."

"You don't have to do this *right now*," he amends.

"I don't know which house is the McInnises'." I blink away from the look Noah gives me and read the numbers on the mailboxes. Hoping for a clue. Or maybe hoping I'll never figure it out and can leave with a clearer conscience for having at least tried.

Noah stops the truck and nods at the house across the street. I don't ask him how he knows which house it is because my tongue has stopped working. I can't form a single thought, remember the reasons I thought it would be good to come here, convince my throat to relax enough to swallow. I reach a shaking hand for the car door handle but can't convince myself to open it.

Warmth covers my other hand.

"There isn't a right or wrong amount of time," Noah says.

I turn back to him and his face is closer than I thought it would be. He can see the way my chest rises and falls with irregular rhythm. The way my eyes are shining.

"You'll be ready when you're ready."

"But—" My voice cracks. I clear my throat and try again. "What if they . . . his family . . . *Steven's* family . . . needs this now? And I'm being selfish and cowardly by not doing it?"

"What if," Noah says, pulling my hand closer to him, pulling all of me away from the door, "you're being selfish by doing this in the first place? What if you're doing this because you need to, not because they need anything from you?"

My chest chills. "Is that what you think?"

"It's just something to consider."

I search his face for something to rail against. Judgment. Disapproval. Superiority. But I can't find what I'm looking for. The set of his mouth is gentle. His eyes are soft. Like he cares how this is affecting me more than anything else.

So I say, "What would *you* do?"

He lets go of my hand and sighs. Takes hold of the steering wheel again. "Probably the same thing you're doing."

I unbuckle my seat belt and open the door.

The fence around the McInnis house is rusted in places,

but the small yard is tidy. The screen door wails when I open it to knock on the wood door behind and I cringe. I can feel Noah's eyes on me. The longer I stand here with no one answering, the more my shoulders tremble.

Run, Kayla.

Don't run.

Finally, I hear footsteps inside and the door cracks open an inch. The woman with the long nose behind it must be Steven's mom.

"I saw you at the hospital," she says before I can open my mouth. "They said you were going to make it and I wondered how that was fair, seeing's how you were the one driving."

My hands want to wrap around my body to defend myself, but I force them to stay at my sides.

"I'm sorry," I say. "I didn't mean for it to happen." It's the truth. Even in the haziness of panic, I didn't really want anyone dead. Not really.

Not *really.*

"Well, it did," she says before closing the door on me.

I stand there, still, on the porch a moment longer, wondering.

And when I turn back to Noah's truck, I still don't know who I did this for.

SPRING

I FINGERED THE PURPLE sequined top, checked the price tag, sucked in a breath through my teeth, and turned away. Then turned back and impulsively pulled the hanger off the rack and pressed the halter against my chest.

"What do you think?" I asked Jen, who flipped through long summer dresses a few feet away. "It'll mean pretty much no spending money for the next two weeks, but . . ."

"But it's amazing and makes your hair freaking glow and would be totally worth it because this is the biggest party of the year?"

"Pretty much exactly that, yeah."

"Do it. Oh! You know it would be cute with those rolled-cuff black shorts you wore in Florida."

I pulled the top away and looked at it critically, imagining the satin-trimmed shorts with it. "Yeah. And that would save me some money. Plus my black heels with the ankle straps."

"Big gold hoops."

"Perfect." I draped the top over my forearm and helped Jen look through dresses. I pulled out a couple, but she shook her head each time. "Stop being difficult," I told her.

"Ugh. I don't know what I want. Just what I don't want."

She held up a cotton dress with an oversized Hawaiian flower print.

I shook my head.

"It swallows me, right?"

"You know what your problem is? You're trying to hide your legs."

"I don't want to look like I'm trying too hard. Like Selena sometimes."

"Ouch, that's cold." I laughed. "But since we're comparing ourselves to our best friends who don't deserve our cattiness, those long dresses are Bean, not you."

"Right. Okay, so new plan. Jen is nicer and she wears . . . this short, fitted silver one?" The dress she held up was little more than a scrap of fabric, one-shouldered with a pattern of metallic-threaded feathers.

"Looks promising. Put it on."

We headed to the fitting rooms and I flopped in a purple faux-leather chair, flipping through an out-of-date fashion magazine while Jen tried the dress on.

"Speaking of feathers." Her disembodied voice drifted over the top of the fitting-room door and I waited for her to go on, but she followed that up with a swear word and I figured she'd caught her earring in her shirt or something. While I waited, I found the quiz in the magazine. It wanted me to know which Disney villain I was. I dug a pen from my purse and started circling my answers. Jen continued, "Jay tracked home a million of them after cleaning your chicken coop last night. Mom was pissed."

"Pissed about the feathers or pissed about cleaning the coop?"

"Both, probably. Her sweet Jaykins wasn't meant for menial labor."

"You can let her know Jay didn't really do anything. He brought eight guys from the team over. All he did was stomp around and give orders like some sort of military commander. They finished in about fifteen minutes."

Your alter ego is: A) A fairy godmother—you have an old soul, B) A dragon—you're ferocious! C) A god—you rule! even if only the underworld, or D) A wealthy eccentric—glam was meant for you.

I tapped the pen against the page a couple of times. "Hey, am I a dragon or a god?"

"What?"

"Never mind." I circled B then added up my points and checked the answer key. "I'm Maleficent." The door to Jen's changing room opened and she stepped out, looking like she would have answered D for that question, all skintight clothing and sparkles and sweeping curls down her back.

I nodded my approval. "Love it."

"Me too." She looked down and read the quiz title. Flopped in my lap. "No, you're definitely not a ruler of the underworld. Besides, I love Maleficent. She's my favorite villain. All morally ambiguous. I mean, her friends didn't invite her to their party. That's just wrong. I'd have been pissed, too."

"No one would dare keep you from their parties. But do I seem morally ambiguous to you?"

She cocked her head to the side and looked at me through the tall mirror in front of her. "No. You're like the opposite of that. *Wholesome.* God, that word was made for you. But there's a first time for everything, right?"

I laughed and shoved Jen off me, then stood and went to pay for my new top.

FALL

I SPEND FRIDAY AFTERNOON in the kitchen with my mom, kneading bread before tackling my homework. Working beside my mom always grants a measure of peace. There is something about her steadiness that calms me, like a gentle springtime sunrise over the land: I know the light's coming and I know it'll warm my bones just as it has every morning of my life.

As I fold and press the dough for Mom's poppy seed rolls, I can't stop thinking about what Noah said about how I might be doing the selfish thing. About how everyone needs a different amount of time to heal. There's a part of me that understands that. But there's more of me—a lot more—that desperately wants to be allowed to be happy. How long do I have to wait to get my life back?

I brush dough off my hands and begin on the dishes, scrubbing fiercely at egg yolk stuck on a plate, trying to release a tightness of anticipation. The pancake breakfast is tomorrow morning. I wonder what Greg Hudson at the real estate office on Third thought when Mom bought three tickets from him last Monday afternoon.

Mom clears her throat at my dishwashing mania, asks how my day was, then reminds me she bought me new jeans.

She pauses and gives the knee-holes in the ones I'm wearing a look.

"But these are so comfy," I tell her sheepishly, rinsing the plate and setting it in the drainer. I wipe my hands on the dish towel. Stuff my hands in my pockets. The ticket is there, bent and fraying around the edges. I've carried it with me since Monday. "Mom, are you disappointed?"

"In the state of the world? It's a messy place nowadays."

I look at her. "In me."

She takes the towel from the counter and starts drying dishes. "When the report came back and I knew you weren't being irresponsible, no."

That report had already come back by the time I'd woken up in the hospital. Blood tests authorized by a mother who was completely sure her daughter hadn't done anything wrong. A surprise welling of tears in the corners of my eyes makes me lower my head. "No. I wasn't."

But then, what *am* I responsible for, really? Seeing what I saw? Allowing myself to be forced into the car? The choice to stop them at any cost? *Any* cost?

I wish the cost hadn't been so high. I wish there had never been a need to pay it at all.

Mom nods and stacks glasses in a cupboard. "It was an accident. A terrible, life-changing accident that will take you a long time to wade through but still an accident."

Sometimes I wonder who it's hardest to lie to. Jen. My mom. Myself.

"What about Dad?"

"What about Dad?" she repeats.

"He's like . . ." I wave a hand around. The faded red roosters on the wallpaper trim stare at me disapprovingly. I'd never noticed before how pissed off those birds look. "Weird. We don't talk like we used to. It's awkward. I feel like he couldn't wait to get me out of here after the accident. I understand why he was ashamed of me. Why people would give him a hard time for being related to the girl who . . ." I swallow.

Mom looks at me around the open cupboard door. "Do you think you're being a little dramatic? He's on your side before anyone else's. We both are. Kayla, we are thrilled to have you home. You can't see that?"

"I guess . . . It's just he was so quick to want me to go to Aunt Bea's. He couldn't wait to get rid—"

"To protect you," she says softly. "Do you think we don't know what people are saying? That we couldn't guess how they would treat you?"

I reach into the fridge for the butter so that Mom can't ˹ the way her words make my chin tremble. Somehow everyone else in this town feels easier than accᴇ my parents sent me away for my own good, not ͭ were embarrassed by me. I don't feel deserving of their good intentions.

When I turn back, Mom gives me an encouraging smile and says, "Okay?" and I half nod. I begin the crust for the lemon meringue pie I'm making for tomorrow's pancake breakfast bake sale table. Mom rolls the lemons across the kitchen counter, laughing when one topples off and bounces off my shoe. A giggle fights its way through my melancholy, and for a moment, I feel like a different person. A little more like the Kayla I used to be. I don't know where or how Mom learned to say the right things at the right time, but I'd be lost without her belief in me.

I pull on jeans, a short-sleeve lace tee, and my black leather flats, pull my hair into a messy bun and stare at myself in the mirror. My eyes look too wide; my cheeks, too pink.

"You look nice," Mom says from the doorway. Her short hair is pulled back with clips, curling around her ears. She has on slacks and a button-up blouse with pictures of dancing vegetables. I'm not sure she ever got over loving to wear cartoon-character nurse's scrubs. "Dad's in the car. I grabbed the pie. Are you ready to go?"

"Yeah." I sweep the ticket off my dresser and close my palm around it.

There is already a line outside Mackleby's Diner when we get there. Dad finds a parking spot a couple of blocks over and we cross the streets in silence. Dad strides ahead of me and Mom, and when he spots Mike Larson, he abandons us to talk about the weather report. Mom and I add ourselves to the rear of the line.

I don't know the people we're standing behind and it's a small blessing.

"Getting warmer," Mom says, as though I want to talk about the weather, too.

I love that this town is so small that sometimes there is nothing else to say.

But when we step inside the diner, I'm reminded how much people in small towns talk about one another. The din of conversation grows softer. The clatter of forks pauses. Selena and some other girls I used to call friends sit at a booth in the back. Selena raises her glass of orange juice as though it's easier to look at me over the top of it than full-on.

Bean is absent. Her parents are here. Her brother is here. The girls I've seen her with since I came back are here. If we're going to pretend nothing happened, where is she?

Mom prods me with the plate she's been holding for a minute already. She knows I need something else to hold, something to balance out the weight of the pi⁄

my focus from the people watching me.

She's so smart.

I shift the lemon meringue pie to r

the plate with my right. Along the ⅂

eggs and bacon rest in heated pans. Behind the pans are members of Mackleby's staff and the homecoming court.

I force myself to look into Jen Brewster's eyes.

"I brought a pie," I say.

She reaches for it from behind the bake sale table and I prepare for our fingers to touch. I crave some connection. A whisper-sweep of our skin, an accidental scratch of her nail on my palm, even. The last time she touched me was to deck me. But she carefully takes the pie plate around the edges, avoiding my hand.

"Thank you." Jen's hair curls around her shoulders and the lace collar on her dress makes her look sweet. But her words are clipped and edged.

My plate nearly slips out of my hand as I fish in my pocket for a dollar bill. I shove it across the table. "I'll buy one of those brownies."

She rolls her eyes and indicates with her hand that I should get one myself.

"Thanks." I bite the inside of my mouth to keep my jaw from shaking. This person I've known and loved my whole life stands across from me as though I'm a stranger.

Someone makes an impatient sound behind me. A gap has opened between me and my mom and I'm holding up the line. I scurry past the bacon and eggs and find myself in ᵗ of the griddle.

or five guys from the football team are here

pouring batter from pitchers onto the hot surface, flipping cakes, laughing at a joke one of them made. In the far corner, a framed photo of Steven McInnis presides over the breakfast, his round face in a perpetual frown. I turn my shoulder to him.

The boys quiet down when I hold my plate out.

Jeremy North leans over a batch of pancakes with his lips pursed. For a second, I think he's about to spit on my plate—

But a strong arm holds him back.

"Chill," Jay Brewster warns him.

Jay's eyes are bright blue over his sharply defined cheeks. Blond hair is slicked back from his forehead. He looks . . . cautious. Over Jay's shoulder, T. J. folds his arms across his chest.

I clear my throat as quietly as possible. It's still too loud.

"Hi, Jay."

It's strange to say his name, the syllables tripping over my tongue. Neither of us is really sure what the other knows, except for the most important thing: neither of us will tell. Somewhere in the lights flickering off our pupils, we communicate.

Keep your mouth shut, Kayla.

Haven't I, Jay?

The diner is quiet. We're all waiting. For something. The tick of the second hand of a clock. The blow of a game-over whistle. A cough, a shattered glass of orange juice.

For a final understanding.

"Welcome home, Kayla," Jay finally says. He breaks out his wide, white smile. "You look amazing. Kansas City agreed with you."

I drop my plate. It hits the ground thickly but doesn't break, bouncing to land right-side up. I mutter a swear word and bend to retrieve it. When I stand again, Jay's still waiting there with that grin and it feels, impossibly, like everything is going to be okay.

But then, why wouldn't it be? I've been back for weeks and I haven't said a thing. It's enough time, apparently, for him to feel confident that I never will tell.

I smile slowly. "Maybe coming home agrees with me."

It's the first thing I can think to say. Something old Kayla would have said. A friendly parry. It feels both natural and completely out of place. Like me in this town.

T. J. nods over Jay's head. "What's up, Kayla?"

My brain filters through every possible response.

Jay must see it: the confusion, the hope. The way his words have nearly knocked me on the floor the way T. J. did the other day in the hall.

Jay chuckles. "Haven't talked for a long time, have we? Not since just after the accident." He shakes his head, looks down, and flips a few pancakes. "What a . . . crazy time that was."

"Yeah." I swallow. "I'm so . . ." *Sorry* seems such an

inadequate thing to say for a life lost, even for a boy who deserved some kind of justice. But not the kind of justice he got.

I know it now. But that night. That night dying meant something different. I even thought, in the wildness of that panic, that Jay and Steven would have killed *me* to ensure I kept quiet.

"It's a tragedy," Jay fills in for me. "The same age as us. Too young."

"I'm sorry," I finally manage, quietly.

"I know. His family knows. It was an accident." He turns slightly. "Jeremy, get Kayla something to drink."

I watch Jeremy pick a clean glass from a stack, lift the lever on the jug next to him, and pass it to me. We all watch. Me and Jay and T. J. and those other boys from the team. From school. And everyone in the diner. From my life before.

"Thanks," I tell Jeremy.

I look back at Jay. He called it an accident. He's smiling at me. Sliding pancakes from the griddle to my plate with a right arm that led our team to the championship last year.

"Jay . . ."

He shakes his head. "It was a long time ago. We need to move on. We can't stop living, you know. People have been incredible. Look around."

I don't look around, but I know the diner's so full people are sitting in chairs against the wall with their plates in their laps. The biggest turnout for the homecoming pancake breakfast fundraiser I've ever seen.

Jay points his spatula into the crowd. "I wouldn't be doing their kindness justice if I stayed angry at you, would I? And my dad's said it a hundred times: forgiveness. So Kayla, I forgive you. I mean, you said before you can't even remember that night. You'll never get that back. That's worse than what I've had to deal with. A hole like that in your memory."

My eyes slide over to Jen. She's waiting, looking at me blankly.

"I don't know what to say," I say.

"Say those are the best pancakes you've ever had and . . ." He shrugs. "We'll call it even."

I look back down the line. The Thompsons, behind me, wait patiently, smiling. The whole diner waits, like they've been waiting their whole lives to hear Jay Brewster confer his grace upon Kayla Martin.

"They look really good." I feel brave enough to give him a tiny laugh.

As I pass near the bake sale table on my way to join my parents, Jen catches my eye.

"Hey, Kayla." She pauses, looking around the diner, reading an invisible script made of smiles, gestures, ebbing tension in the air. "We already sold your pie."

I look at the table, and sure enough, the lemon meringue pie is gone.

* * *

The breeze feels like a baptism.

"It's been so hot," Jen complains, coming up beside me on Spark, one of the new horses at her family's therapy facility. She pulls off her hoodie and throws it on the ground.

Just when we thought autumn had sunk its claws in completely, summer swooped in for one last, desperate week.

"Stop complaining. It'll be freezing again too soon. Ugh. Do not want." I shield my eyes with my hand and look at my best friend.

My best friend.

I've repeated the phrase in my head a million times since the pancake breakfast. Since the few moments before the first bell rang at school the next Monday, when Jen came up to me, gathered me in a hug in front of everyone and said, "I'm so glad you're back." When Selena followed, knowing a hug would erase the cruel things she said to me, the way she pushed me at Toffey's and at the powder-puff game. We all knew I wanted my old life back badly enough to forget everything.

I've repeated it out loud, too. When I can hardly believe in the truth of it. My best friend.

"You don't know how sorry I am," I'd said to her that Monday, still enfolded in her embrace.

"I think I do. It was hard having you gone. But now you're here and everything will go back to normal. I'll save you a seat in Schroeder's class," she'd promised before we parted.

And she had. So had Selena. In the classes we shared, at our old lunch table, with my old friends back on my side again, in her car when she gave me rides home from school. I could pretend no time had passed for us.

I do pretend that.

And it makes me happier than I've been in a long time.

This morning, one week after the breakfast, she got me on my horse again.

"I know you think you'll never ride like you used to, but you still belong up here."

I greeted Caramel Star with a heavy heart, but her deep, dark eyes seemed to see through me, understanding that even though our old life of competitions and trophies was over, I still needed her to feel free, to feel home. We soared across Jen's back fields and my heart soared, because I felt like my life was finally getting back to normal again.

Now, Jen and I work together breaking in the new horse while we wait for Selena to call so we can go dress shopping for the homecoming dance next weekend.

I lead the sweet bay around the pen while Jen sits in the saddle. She looks beautiful up there. An equestrian goddess, even though she's in ragged jeans and a T-shirt, not her competition blazer and smart black helmet.

My best friend.

"If the heat holds, maybe we can get strapless dresses,"

she says, letting the reins dangle over her thighs.

I laugh and kick up some dust. "Like we weren't going to anyway."

When Jen smiles, a deep dimple pokes her right cheek. Her eyes sparkle. Her hair glows. That might just be the way the sun backlights her head, but it might also be the way I view her now. As something precious I almost lost forever.

I lead the horse out of the enclosure and lean against the white board fence while Jen puts her away. It's warm enough for short sleeves during the day, but still cool once night falls. I grip my upper arms. The grasses sprawling out behind the barns are dotted with late-season dandelions. Squirrels zip from tree to tree in preparation for a long winter.

The air smells fresh. Light. The back of my neck warms. Contentment is almost thorough.

Then a door slams. Jay stands on the back deck, squinting in our direction. His shirt is gray, almost matching the color of the house, with its charcoal siding and white trim. Jay's been . . . cool with me since the pancake breakfast.

"Jen," he calls. "Phone."

Jen appears next to me, drying her hands on the front of her jeans. "That'll be Selena."

After dress shopping, we plan on settling in for a sleepover, like we always used to. Before I left, it would be four of us snuggling under layers of blankets. Now, as we walk back to the house to talk to Selena on the phone, I want to hear Jen's side of the story. How four became three. "What changed with us, Jen?"

She pulls her hair out of the ponytail and runs her fingers through to loosen it while she thinks.

"You and me?" she says, and I want to correct her. No, me and you and Selena and *Bean*, but she rushes on before I can say anything, as though her feelings are a river undammed. "The worst part of what you did was leaving, you know. I mean, what happened to Steven was horrible. But it was an accident. Leaving made you seem . . . guilty. Like you did something wrong. On purpose. Or there was some secret you were running from. Or even like . . . you didn't trust me." Her chin quivers, and when she turns to me, I see her eyes swimming with hurt. Betrayal. "That's the first time I've said that. Like, realized that's what really hurt. You didn't have enough faith in me that I would be here for you. After everything we've been through. How could you think I would turn my back on you like that?"

I blink rapidly. "I just thought you'd be angry. Jay's your brother. And your mom . . ."

"I am *not* my mother." She bites her lip, her eyes flickering to the windows at the back of her house.

I know Jen and the tangle of decisions she has to make: what to do to gain favor with her parents, what to do to pull away and show them she doesn't care what they think. It makes me wonder, even more, what she knows.

"You and me, we're basically sisters. Or something better. And yeah, he's my brother, but he walked away that night, you know? You wouldn't think it, the way he's been babied. His oh-so-precious arm is fine after all that physical therapy."

"I'm pretty sure you're the only one who thinks that."

"Jay wasn't a perfect QB before the accident. People *love* to forget that. Remember . . ." Her voice falters. She starts to say something but pauses again and shakes her head, as though she's thinking of one memory, but changes to something different at the last second. "Remember when he got sacked twenty yards back from the line of scrimmage last year? What a mess. I guess . . . now they have someone other than him to blame when he screws up. Easier to get pissed at you than at their god. But that will go away."

Jen shrugs, but the gesture can't erase the responsibility the town has put on my shoulders. And it wasn't just Jay. A boy *died* in that accident. That lingers, even if he wasn't the star of the team. Even if he wasn't from a wealthy, influential family like the Brewsters.

"Okay, but . . ." I turn the conversation to what happened with Bean when I was gone. "What's going on with Bean?"

Jen's fingers freeze and fall to rest on the back of her neck. She breathes through her nose. After a long exhale, she slowly unfolds her hands. "Bean . . . changed over the summer. Found new friends and ditched us," she says carefully.

"Weird," I say, and there are a million reasons why it's

weird and almost as many reasons why it's not.

"It all started the night of the party, really."

"It did?"

Jen looks at me, considering.

I let my eyes widen slightly, just enough to be curious but not guilty of knowing more than I should. They don't convey the way my blood vessels are shrinking, tightening and depriving my brain of oxygen in anticipation of her next words. Of learning what Jen knows about that night.

"I almost forgot. You don't remember." She says that last bit forcefully, as though commanding something I've already proven I'm willing to give.

I swallow and look at the ground. Here, the dirt of the ring and broken growth around the barns gives way to the lush, thick grass of the Brewsters' yard.

"Right," I say.

Dad's driving in on his tractor, heading to the house for dinner. I finish pulling out one of the rusted screws holding in the old oarlocks and turn off the drill.

"How's repairs?" he asks as he shuts off the engine and climbs down.

"Really good. The new oarlocks just came in and I finished the exterior sanding this morning." I tick off my accomplishments on my fingers. "I have to finish the interior sanding, but all the seats and skeleton make it take longer."

"I'd help more if I wasn't so busy."

If he wasn't trying to avoid me. "It's all right. I got this."

He surprises me when he says, "How about we do that sanding this weekend?"

"I think I'd like that." I clear my throat. "But . . . probably not? I have a lot going on this weekend. Don't think there'll be time."

"That's right. Last homecoming game of high school for you. It's a big night." Dad picks up a dirty rag from the seat of the tractor then wipes the back of his arm across his forehead. "Kayla," he says. "Can I ask you something?"

I look up at Dad, at his serious face. I don't really want to answer questions from him. Maybe because I can't predict what they'll be. Or maybe because what I need from him isn't questions but an explanation. Did he really send me away because he was scared for me or because he was ashamed of me? I sigh. "I'm not sure I'll know the answer."

"Well, that's fair warning. But I'm going to ask anyway." He pauses. "How did you end up in a car with Jay Brewster and Steven McInnis?"

I frown and twist a piece of hair around my finger. I stuff my hands in my back pockets and squint. "Jen and I had a fight that night. About where she's going to college. And how I don't want to go with her." I pause, but Dad keeps folding his rag into fourths like I haven't said anything at all. A lone hawk circling overhead shrieks at us. "After that

I walked away to get some space."

"So you went for a drive." *In someone else's car*, he doesn't say.

"I don't . . ." I swallow and Dad picks up on my hesitation, eager to close a little bit more the gap that grew between us after that night.

"Must feel pretty bad not remembering."

I let him believe that's the reason I didn't finish my sentence. I want that gap closed, too.

"Maybe I don't . . . want to," I hedge.

Dad looks down at the rag. "What I really mean . . . what I really want to know . . . is if you're okay. Just . . . Steven wasn't always the finest character, from what I'd always understood." I follow Dad to the shed, where he tosses the rag atop a pile of dirty ones. "And Jay Brewster likes to test what he can get away with sometimes. A boy like that will."

I stiffen. Pull a splinter of loose wood from the corner of Dad's workbench.

"You're one of the few people around here who thinks that."

"You'd think that, wouldn't you? With the way some folks get so caught up in that team. But this is a whole town of people and we're not all the same. I know that. That's why I made sure you went to Bea's."

I dig the splinter under my fingernail, wincing at the sharp stab of pain. "Because of how people treated you after that night. Because of what I did. Who I hurt. I'm sorry, Dad."

"It was never about me. I should have told you right off the bat why I wanted you to go to your Aunt Bea's. I'm the one who's sorry. For not making that clear."

For the first time since I've been home, I look my dad in the eye. The truth of what he's saying is written there. And the realization that I needed his explanation and apology all along is written in my heart. "Thank you. For wanting to protect me."

He laughs a little and I duck my head, realizing how my words sound. Like I doubted him. But he lets it go. "Coming in for dinner?"

"Yeah," I say. "I just want to finish getting the oarlocks off. I only have one more to go."

Dad nods and I pick up the drill again, pressing the trigger over and over again until I've drowned out the sound of that night.

SPRING

CALEB FOUND ME DURING my free period on Thursday, sitting on the hill and doodling in an old notebook.

"What are you doing here?" I said to him. Yesterday was the last day for seniors, and the way he'd been dismantling everything in his bedroom and talking nonstop about the summer camp counselor job he'd scored made it clear to our entire family that he couldn't wait to get out of town.

"You should ditch the last couple of periods and hike Point Fellows with me," Caleb said. He motioned to my sneakers. "You look ready to go."

"There's a party in my French class next period," I said. "Madame Lechat said she was bringing cheese and pastries."

"So? I'm leaving soon. You would turn down time spent with your favorite brother for *cheese*? I'm hurt."

"You're my only brother," I said.

But I squinted in the general direction of Point Fellows. The air had that soft spring afternoon quality to it, when the rays of the sun were blurred into a watercolor painting by dust and dampness. The sunset, when it came, would be layer upon layer of lavender and pink and orange. Caleb headed out in a week. Our moments together were limited.

I closed my notebook and stood. "Okay."

I followed Caleb to his truck, tossing my backpack in
before climbing up. He'd scrubbed the truck spotless a few
days ago and it smelled almost sickly sweet inside; a purple
deodorizer hung from the rearview mirror. A swift pain
struck my chest. Caleb was a notorious slob. Cleaning his
truck was a statement of change.

I watched Caleb as we sat behind a tractor that had
backed up cars five deep on the road to Point Fellows. It
looked like he'd gone several days without handling a razor
and months since getting a haircut. Still, his jaw looked
sharper, and he'd taken to wrinkling his forehead so that
a couple of lines emerged across it. Looking at my brother
ready to head off into the world made me feel oddly young.

The tractor finally pulled to the shoulder of the road and
all the cars behind it zoomed by. We raced down a road that
hardly saw any other traffic, and when we pulled into the
parking lot at the trailhead, knew we would have time to kill
before sunset. I ambled behind Caleb for the first few hundred yards, kicking pebbles at the heels of his shoes, then we
slowed as the incline grew steeper.

At the clearing at the end of the trail, I picked the first
opened dandelions of the season and sat next to Caleb on the
edge of the bluff, our feet dangling over, and blew the wispy
seeds out over the river and valley below.

He took several long, deep breaths like he was filtering
all of home through his lungs, holding on to what he loved

and letting go of what he couldn't keep, and said, "I'm going to miss you, Kayla Koala." I smiled briefly at the nickname only he called me. A reference to the mangled-by-love koala stuffed animal Caleb had given me when I was a toddler. "I'm going to miss a lot about this place." He jingled his keys in his left palm. I relieved another dandelion of its seeds. "There are some things I won't miss." And I thought about how far we were from major airports and our lack of dance clubs and how there were only so many girls in town. All the things I was sure Caleb wouldn't miss. "Small towns are funny places," he went on. "Filled with people who know everyone. No places to hide."

I gave him a look. "What have you been reading lately?"

"We're the same." He went on as though I hadn't said anything. "We love this place so hard. Our lungs are as full of the dirt of this place as they are the air." He looked at me, his eyebrows narrowing as he considered what to say next. The dancing smile I always associated with Caleb was missing. "But I'm glad to be leaving."

This intense side of Caleb gave me chills. I crushed the dandelion stems between my fingers and the bluff's dry dirt. It was hard to tell if he was telling me how happy he was to leave because he wanted to make his leaving, his changing our family dynamic, easier on me and Mom and Dad, or because he needed to make it easier on himself. Put distance between himself and a place he loved as much as I did. Make leaving bearable.

He unclenched his jaw and softened his hand enough that his keys fell out and onto the ground. An old Caleb smile fought its way through. "New adventures, right? I'll miss you, Kayla Koala," he repeated. "You've always kept me good. When I think about doing something, I ask myself, what would my little sister think of me if I do this? What kind of example am I setting?"

I smiled. "That's shocking because you've done some stupid things."

"Just think of the stupid things I haven't done!"

"Like what?"

"I don't want to sully your pristine memory of me by telling."

I snorted. "I have a few choice words to describe you if you'd like to hear—"

"Hey, now," he interrupted. He nudged my shoulder with his and I had to throw my arm out to keep my balance. I pushed back, but he just bit off a laugh and scratched at his cheek stubble. "I wouldn't believe what you'd say anyway. I know how awesome you really think I am."

I gave him a soft smile. He was leaving soon. "What makes you think my descriptions wouldn't have been awesome?"

"Aw, Koala." A flush ran up his neck. For a quiet moment, we watched the sky change. Caleb broke the moment when he took a long breath and I looked at him. His shoulders were tense, but he dropped his chin and his whole body slumped with it. "I'm not always awesome, though."

The tone of his voice kept me from cracking another joke. Instead, I waited.

He raised his head again. A light flickered in his eyes. The same hazel mishmash of green and gray and yellow as mine. We could see a long way from the top of Point Fellows, but he seemed to be looking even farther than was possible. Into another place. Another time. "Have you ever been in a situation when you weren't sure you did the right thing?"

I shrugged. Pushed a strand of hair out of my mouth. Tasted the bitterness of dandelion stem on my lip. "I guess."

He shook his head. "No, I mean . . . a time when maybe it was easier to believe you *weren't* supposed to do something even though you probably should have? And you convinced yourself inaction was the same as not doing harm when really . . ." His fingers fidgeted along the seams of his jeans, but my body was still. There was more he wanted to say, something important he needed to relieve himself of, maybe. But the funny thing was that, just like he said, I wasn't sure I wanted to hear it, even though I probably should want to. It was the way his secret, if that's even what it was, felt so heavy.

"Are Mom and Dad okay?"

"Yeah," he said quickly. "They're fine." He shook his head, swung his legs back onto solid ground, and held a hand out to help me to my feet. "It's nothing. What I'm trying to say is . . . keep cool while I'm gone, okay?"

I stared at Caleb's hand for a beat before taking it. There was something new about Caleb. Something damaged. I flipped through the events of the past few months, trying to think of when the change began but couldn't pinpoint a specific moment.

"Don't worry. I'll keep being the superhero," I said. "Fighting for what's right and good."

"Koala suit and cape and trusty steed and all?"

I laughed, but Caleb didn't join in. "Something like that. But yeah, you can count on me to be the good one."

The good one.

FALL

I HELP MOM CLEAR off the dinner table and then head over to Toffey's to meet up with Jen and Selena.

Tuesday is open mike night at Toffey's and the pace is brisk. I grab a tiny table in the corner. Bean's here, with a few other girls, including the curly-haired one from my first day back at school. I chew the inside of my cheeks as Jen slides into the chair next to me. She frowns when she sees me looking at Bean's table. Selena catches Jen's eye and just as quickly looks away and I feel a stab of annoyance. Have I not proven myself enough?

"I'll grab us something," Selena says. "What do you want?"

"Mocha. Tell them not to be stingy with the whipped cream," Jen says.

They both look at me. But over Selena's shoulder I see Bean fiddling with the watch around her left wrist and working her jaw, her gaze moving from me to Jen and back.

I hate that I don't know what she's thinking. That I don't know so much of what she's been thinking. Months' worth of thoughts. A hummingbird hovers in my chest. I didn't expect to see Bean here. As though normal, everyday life couldn't, shouldn't go on after that night. As though going for coffee, laughing with a friend, being *out*, is only for people without secrets weighing them down.

I stand. "Actually, I need to go."

"But we just got here." Jen gapes at me.

"Yeah, so just tell me what you want before the line gets longer," Selena says.

"I'm not thirsty anymore."

As if anyone gets coffee because they're thirsty. My knuckles knock against the table. One finger hits a dried-out piece of gum.

"I forgot that . . . at home I have to . . ." But I can't think of an excuse that would get me out of here. The idea that I want to run away from the things I've sacrificed so much to get back in my life tears at me.

"I want you to stay." Jen's voice is soft but I can count the layers of meaning in it.

Stay because I want to hang out with you.

Stay because you owe me.

Stay because there are still things to prove to me, to all of us.

"I'll just get you a mocha, too, okay, Kayla?" Selena says. She pauses for a beat before turning away without waiting for my answer.

I watch her retreat and notice the taut shoulder muscles revealed by her tank top.

My eyes drift from Selena back to Bean.

Bean doesn't know. *Can't* know. But in her expression I

see it all: that she knows I saw, that there is still space to make things right.

If I were only willing to give up my home.

I hold my breath until the room spins. This isn't how it's supposed to happen. What happened that night was supposed to stay in the past. I thought that was what everyone wanted. Once I make up with my friends, we are supposed to stay made up. Things go back to normal, to the way they were.

"Are you going to sit down?" Jen says. She looks at me, picks up her phone to check her messages.

The coffee shop goes quiet but only for me.

Terry Brady still reads a poem. The espresso machine grinds and churns. Other kids in our class get up and down from their seats. It feels like there are too many people, too many eyes watching me.

No, just two eyes.

Across the room, Bean is looking at me, still. Even from across the room, I can tell that her lips are pressed together so hard that they're outlined by a little white line. Suddenly, I'm not sure about what I've done or who I am. An annoying trill begins in my ears. The chair nearly topples over when I push back. "No . . . I have to go."

"What is wrong with you?"

"I don't feel good."

Jen sighs. "I'll give you a ride home."

"I have my bike."

"Put it in the back of my car."

Jen knows. She has to know everything. Jen and Selena and Bean. Jay. My parents. Is there anyone who can't see the truth in the terrible darting of my gaze, in the way my hands tremble?

Jen reaches for me. Her look of concern is pure, a best friend's. "You *do* look sick. Your face is splotchy. Let's get you home."

Her touch is soft as petals. Her touch stings like wasp bites.

I pull out my phone. "I'm calling my mom to get me. I don't want you to get sick, too." I hold up the phone to my ear and walk out to make a fake call.

I dodge off the road and into dirt, drop my bike, and use my feet. The truth about cornfields is that they're hard to run through. The corn's planted tightly to maximize acreage and the stalks are mean and stubborn, unwilling to bend to a person's will. The leaves are sharp. A slice from one feels like a paper cut times a million.

Still, I push through and they crack and snap under the pressure of my shoes like tiny bones. Every time one breaks, a pain shoots into my ankle.

The night air smells like this sweet, new corn so I breathe it in as I run, and it comforts me and fuels my anger at the same time.

I wish I hated this smell.

But I love it and I love this town and I want to love everyone the way I used to love them. I want for them to love me the same way, too.

I just need to keep running.

And I can't wonder about whether or not people know I remember what happened at Jen's party last spring. Because then I not only have to question the kind of person *I* am, but the kind of people Jen and Selena are. So many people in this town. I run fast and I run far to keep my mind away from those questions.

I reach a dirt road and dart across it, belatedly hearing the honk. A truck slams on its brakes, raising a cloud of dust and rock. I am frozen in the road like a deer.

The driver's door opens and a worn pair of jeans and faded T-shirt appear through the cloud.

"Why are you always in *places*?" I ask Noah, fighting back a swelling urge to run to him. "Places I am? You used to be invisible."

"I watched you leave Toffey's."

"I didn't know you were there."

"Then I guess I still am invisible."

I swallow hard and walk to him, staying on the other

side of his still-open door. My palms on the window frame steady me.

Pieces of Noah's dirty blond hair blow back from his face. Behind him, the sky has taken on the colors of fire.

"I want to be invisible," I whisper.

"Then get in."

Noah moves aside so I can climb into his truck. I slide across the seat and watch as he gets in and settles himself behind the steering wheel.

We don't say anything. Not yet. We drive around, looking for a place we can both talk and feel safe. A fairy-tale land.

We pull over at an abandoned house on the south side of town. The porch has half fallen off and there are old, yellowed curtains in the windows, drifting like ghosts, but I go in anyway. There are candle stubs and empty bottles in the corners of the front room. Overhead, a wide hole in the ceiling affords me a view of the darkening sky.

Noah follows me, a guitar in his left hand. His keys in his right.

"I thought you played the banjo," I say.

His lips turn up. "I can only play one instrument?"

"Play whatever you want. Play all the instruments. Play me something."

"That's why I brought it in." I realize his voice is husky. Always? Or just at night. Just when he's about to play music. Just when he's sheltered by invisibility.

I pick a spot on the floor and lower myself, cross-legged.

He sits across from me, just a few feet away, cradling the guitar across his lap. His fingers move like ghosts across the strings as he thinks about what to play. The silence between us is comfortable, but then he looks up and gives me a small smile and suddenly, out of nowhere and everywhere at once the silence is charged, trembling with possibility, with things I've seen and not seen, with the way he's been near me lately and the way he's granted me space and the way he's been careful. Careful like he understands what it is to be delicate. A struggling thing just planted in its home.

His ghost fingers finally make contact with the strings and he begins to play. Every strum, every chord change, every gritty slide across the guitar, amps up the electricity in the air until my breath slows and deepens. I breathe lower, from my belly, from my legs, and from my reconstructed ankle.

While Noah plays, I study his profile. His neck is long, his jawline strong. Some of his features are his dad's: clean-shaven Midwestern guy, while others must also belong to his dark-eyed mom. They blend in a uniquely beautiful way, so different from the typical boy from around here. I know it means something to him to be different, to look different, to do different things from everyone else.

In an instant, I hate everyone who's ever made life diffi-cult for him, who's teased him for creating music rather than being an athlete. Who's called him a name behind his back while smiling to his face because his skin doesn't go pale like everyone else's in the winter.

"It's beautiful," I say.

His eyes flick up to meet mine.

"Your playing."

"Thank you." He strums a few more times then says, "Things will go back to normal, you know. It takes time, but it will be like before for you. If that's what you want."

He clears his throat and loses the easy rhythm but catches it again quickly.

I almost tell him I don't know what I want. Not anymore.

"Like they were before," I whisper instead. "You have no idea."

And I almost tell him everything, but I don't. Maybe because I'm scared he'll hate me if he knows the truth.

Instead I say, "Remember when we were little and your family came over sometimes for barbecues?"

"I didn't think you remembered that."

I run the hem of my shirt between my fingers. I remember everything. Some things I don't want him to know about. Others mark us, make old friends of us. Connect me to him in a way I only just started wanting.

He keeps playing.

"Sometimes we'd have them in the late autumn," I say.

"More time to hang out after the harvest is finished."

"It got dark earlier. You always stayed long enough to watch the stars with me."

Noah doesn't say anything for a minute. The silence feels long. Old memories feel good.

"I named a star after you," he says.

My back straightens. "Which one?"

His chest shudders under a soft chuckle. "How would I remember which one? It was a long time ago. Stars were different then."

"Everything was different then." I tip my chin back and stare at the night sky through the ceiling hole, searching for the winking spot he would have given my name.

None of them looks right. That childhood moment of naming the particles of the universe feels too far away, and even if I reach my arm for thousands of miles, I know I can't touch the children we once were. "The stars were different once upon a time. Brighter. Now they've lost their luster."

"You haven't," he says, and strums again.

SPRING

I STOPPED BY MY house to grab my new top before heading over to Jen's the Friday after school let out. I passed by Caleb's room as I walked down a hallway that was covered with photos of the two of us, in varying thicknesses of brown wood frames. Caleb's legs stuck out from under his bed. Dad sat opposite in the chair at his desk, wrapping computer cords into neat bundles.

I paused with my shoulder against the frame of his door, remembering how Mom's been wanting to paint the trim white for ages. Farmers don't have a lot of time.

"Hey, Dad. Caleb, you're coming tonight, right?"

"To Jen's?" His reply was muffled by his mattress.

"To Jen's."

"Nah."

"Why not?"

"Trying to clean up the last of this. Get packed. Leave Monday."

"Can't you do all that tomorrow?"

"Nah."

"Come on. You should come over for the last time. A bunch of people will be there. Say your good-byes and all that."

"You should go," Dad added. "There's not much here to finish up."

Caleb's palms reached back and he slid himself out into the middle of the room. A dust bunny clung to the edge of his hair.

"I'm just not in the mood, you know?"

I took a long look at my brother. The kind I hadn't for a while. Maybe never had. There was something new around his eyes. A seriousness I hadn't noticed before. Caleb was always the energized, goofy big brother who made everyone laugh. But now he looked older. He looked like an outsider.

"If you change your mind," I said. "You know where to find me."

He nodded.

FALL

I STAND IN THE entrance to first period math and scan the faces inside. Pete. T. J. No Noah yet.

Selena comes up behind me. "What are you doing?"

I clutch my books to my chest and turn to her.

"I'm tired." I press the corner of my math textbook into my palm to keep emotions at bay.

But Selena sees everything. "Come on."

We tiptoe out of the school and head for the girls' bathroom out by the fields, where no one bothers to go except when there's an evening game on. The mirrors are old and scratched out here but clear enough for me to stare listlessly at myself: round eyes, snub nose, long blond bangs. I stare so long that I cease making sense—the outline of my head, my body blurring into the fluorescent lights above me.

"Can't sleep?" Selena pulls lip balm from her bag and sweeps her lips with it, ending with a pucker and a popping noise at her reflection.

"Something like that." I sigh. It's not something I've told Aunt Bea or my parents because I don't want them to think I'm regressing after having settled into a better sleep pattern once again in Kansas City, but it has been hard to sleep since I got home. I lie awake at night and hear things out my window, under my bed, in my mind. When I close my eyes, I see things like twin flashes of light and ragged-edged glass. I play over and over again what Noah said about my luster and how I haven't lost it and decide I can't believe that to be true. There is too much darkness for me to shine anymore. No matter what Noah says. No matter how I feel when I'm with him. Because of this feeling I'm having right now, when I'm with Selena or when I'm with Jen or around Jay or my parents or, most of all, when I feel Bean is watching me.

I scratch my elbow. "I just think about how much has changed between us. I changed things when I left."

Selena leans against the sink and snaps her bag shut. "Yeah, but . . . things were going to change anyway, right? I mean, we're all going to different colleges and after that . . ." She shrugs. "I never really saw me or Jen coming back here for good, you know? Not like you. The way you love this place. Everyone else will be heading off to other things. New things."

I place a hand on my shoulder and rub my thumb along my collarbone. "I hate thinking about everyone leaving."

I hate thinking about what it takes to stay.

"It's gonna happen. Lots will change." Her eyes flick to me then away. "Lots changed that night."

Her voice sounds so far away that I start. Study her face. She looks away to play with the keychain dangling from her bag strap. It's a Shrinky Dink turtle she made years ago.

She used to have one half of a silver BFF heart on the ring, too. It's gone now and the bag doesn't look right without it. *She* doesn't look right, never walking with Bean. Laughing with her.

Every time I see a person, a part of this town I used to know, something doesn't look *right*.

I wanted to ask Selena about Bean the last time the two of us stayed over at Jen's house. Selena brought a bottle of vodka and some juice and she and Jen had a few drinks. I sipped at one the whole night, too afraid of what someone might say or think if they walked in. If Jay walked in. If his mom did.

We didn't say much to each other when I was over at the Brewsters', me and Jen's mom.

But Selena got tipsy enough to want to dance around in her bra and underwear. To spill at length about this college guy she saw on the weekends sometimes.

I wanted her to tell me more. Not about the college guy, but about what happened with her and Bean.

Something held me back. The way Jen and Selena both always tensed up when Bean was around. The way they'd laid the blame at Bean's feet when, really, ditching people was not the way Bean ever operated.

Now, though, being alone with Selena gives me an opening.

"What happened with you and Bean?" I ask.

"Me and Bean," Selena repeats. She rummages through her bag again, this time bringing out a handful of Starburst. She tosses an orange one and a pink one to me.

We unwrap and chew them. Mine stick in my teeth. I'm glad for something to do. I don't entirely want to hear what she has to say. What she knows.

Finally, she says, "Bean had some stuff to say about that night."

I dig a piece of candy from my molar with my fingernail. She doesn't seem to notice the way my back has stiffened. "Like what? What could Bean say that would change the two of you?"

"You say that like it's impossible for best friends to change." She tips her chin at me. The example in front of her. "Anyway, I can't say. Can't speak for Bean. You'll have to talk to her about it. Just . . . don't tell Jen you're snooping around."

It's as though Selena *wants* me to talk to Bean. To discover something.

Selena tosses her candy wrappers on the concrete ground and fixes her bangs in the mirror.

I lean back against a stall and read the writing engraved on it.

Tory Worth is a ho.
Kat and Lance 4eva.
P.M., T.F., I.Y. Class of '06 BFFs

When I look up again, Selena's finger has paused on the center of her forehead and she's looking at me through the mirror with narrowed eyes.

I open another candy and stuff it in my mouth, startling when I accidentally bite the side of my tongue.

"Careful, Kayla," she says, picking her bag off the ground and reaching for the door.

When Selena decides to head back to the main building, I tell her I'm going to stay out here a little longer. She enfolds me in a tight, quick hug and says she'll take notes for me in our next class.

I stand at the entrance to the bathrooms and watch her stride across the baseball field. She's shorter than me or Jen, but she walks faster than either of us.

I wait for the next PE class to come out, but it's freshmen and they stop at the running track to time their miles, and I'm still alone. A bunch of birds are picking at the days-old remains of chili fries hidden under the bleachers. They scatter when I sit on the ground with my back to the bleachers but approach again cautiously when I don't make any sudden movements.

Selena's words echo in my head, and I can't decide if they were meant as a suggestion or as a warning. Because they sounded like a warning, with the way she bit them off and looked at me hard as she spoke. But if they *were*, then that means there's something some people know and that some people don't.

Or shouldn't.

And I *really* don't want there to be.

I finally feel like I've come home. Jen and Selena are on my side. Jay doesn't hesitate to join our group as we walk down the school halls. I feel the protective embrace of being near my mom again. And although the newness of being here again stings now, there's a part of me that can see beyond today to a time that will feel better and completely normal again.

At this moment, however, I ache. For the divide between us, for Selena's having to use the word "snooping."

I knew it would be hard to come home. *Hard.*

Hard doesn't begin to describe it. When I decided to come home, I thought finding my place again would be like a steady, dependable climb up a slowly rising mountain path—but the reality is that the journey home has been full of peaks and low valleys. Reconciliations and retrogrades. Inconsistencies and changes that leave me brittle like glass. Too easy to shatter.

I should have known it would be like this. Even if I am eventually successful in ignoring it. The way I've chosen to ignore the way I think Bean looks at me, like she hopes I'll admit I remember and say something. The certainty that, were I in her position, I'd have dumped my old friends, too.

The knowledge that this town, this place, can never be for me what it once was, because I've seen a dark side of it I hadn't known existed before that party. I'm fighting against a current and it's only a matter of time before I tire out and let it pull me under.

I know this. I know it. And I keep swimming. What is wrong with me?

I pick a few dandelions from a patch struggling through the ground next to me. Their yellow blossoms are cheerful. Over the summer, there were enough in our yard for Mom to fill our pantry with dandelion syrup and dandelion jam. This morning, the floral syrup was on my pancakes.

The third period bell rings, and I stand and brush off the back of my jeans. I walk over to the football stadium.

It's a special place, this stretch of bleachers, emerald-green grass, and recycled-rubber running track. Students and alumni squish into the seats until people are half dangling off the edges then continue spreading out on the ground from there with blankets and picnics and toddlers digging for bugs. People have first kisses under the bleachers, share nachos with plastic-cheese sauce with their best friends, listen to the band play big, brassy songs.

I climb the bleachers halfway and sit, staring out at the field as though there's a game on now.

Our high school crest is freshly painted at the fifty yard line in preparation for the homecoming game. Two years ago,

Jay Brewster threw a sailing, forty-yard pass from there, right into the hands of his receiver, and brought glory to this town. He took the team all the way to the state championships with a golden arm that obeyed his every command. And then he did it again last year. He expected one more repeat before heading to one of the colleges clamoring for his presence.

All that and he keeps up a solid GPA, has a strong jawline to offset his bright blue eyes, and volunteers at the elementary school. A college team's dream. A true golden boy.

Everyone knows he'll go all the way. Be a small-town kid hitting it big in the pros. We'll all have something to tell our grandkids about when we visit his display at the Hall of Fame someday. He is everything a nice boy in a nice town in the Midwest should be. Can be. In every way.

I stamp my feet. A metallic sound rings out, fading somewhere in the hills.

"I'm sorry, Jay," I tell a thin cloud over my head. "I'm *sorry* for what I did. But mostly, I'm sorry for what you did. You destroyed everything I believed in."

I clomp down the bleachers, kick at the white line at the edge of the field. Chew on a strand of hair and stare at the sky for a while, thinking about what I still believe. But I can't come up with anything. Then I walk home.

My brother's truck is coming up the dirt road in the distance, flinging gravel off his back tires at the poor, straggling corn planted nearest the road. It's Wednesday, and he probably has classes at Missouri State tomorrow and Friday, but a small-town homecoming is a big deal and he's not going to miss it. The last time I saw Caleb was the day of Jen's party. When I woke up in the hospital, he'd already left for his summer job in the Ozarks. I wonder if he'll look different. I wonder if he'll look at me differently.

It will be a little while until his truck finishes navigating the bends in the road and pulls up by our house. Instead of rushing into the house to meet him, I climb into my boat, pull the air filter over my nose and mouth and my head-phones over my ears, and start up the sander.

Sanding the exterior was a quick project, my hands guid-ing the machine across the gently sloping surfaces easily. Inside, though, the skeleton of the boat is exposed and it takes patience to sand each piece protruding from the outer boards. How simple it would be to be a boat, with a strong, visible interior and an exterior that can be beautified with nothing more than a blast of rough paper.

Music blares through my headphones, loud enough to be heard over the sander's buzzing. There is noise and sawdust and there are muscles in achingly strange positions and there is the anticipation of seeing my brother. But through it all there is a small opening for those thoughts to break through. When I think about Bean, my wrist shakes the sander and there is a loud screech.

I push up the protective goggles and aim a heavy blow of air and tears at the patch I just sanded, realizing with a start that I am done. This boat is ready for a first coat of primer. For a new life.

I replace the sandpaper with a new piece, wrap the cord around the machine, and set it next to the boat.

By the time I get back to the house, my brother's voice has filled every corner of every room and our mom looks like she's about to cry, holding tightly to her boy. He releases her and bounds through the kitchen when he hears the back screen door slam shut and, before I can shout a welcome, scoops me in his arms, lifts me off my feet, and hollers: "Kayla Koala!"

I giggle despite myself at the old nickname. It's such a reminder of who we used to be. It's an assurance that, after everything, Caleb is here and he's my brother and he's on my side.

"Put me down," I protest.

His energy, like always, brightens the room.

When Caleb drops me to my feet, we grin at each other, taking in how we both have changed since before the summer.

His hair's shorter than before, the waves that used to tickle the back of his neck neatly trimmed to above his ears, and his hazel eyes are clearer and brighter. Same old jeans and T-shirt, which reveals the half-sleeve tattoo that almost gave our parents dual heart attacks back in the day.

A lump catches in my throat. He looks so happy.

"You're filthy," he says.

I laugh. "You're ugly."

Caleb reaches for my head, but I duck under his arm while Mom stands and tells us to knock it off and get in the dining room. Dinner smells amazing. It's Caleb's favorite: pot roast, potatoes, and green beans. While we stuff our faces, Caleb tells us about school. I can tell he's sugar-coating it for Mom and Dad, but I know I'll get the details from him later.

After we finish cleaning up dinner dishes, I decline dessert and escape out the front door, sitting on the porch steps, waiting for the sun to set. Dragonflies buzz around my head, their constant chatter lulling me into a half-nap.

I press my hands gently over my face and close my eyes. Caleb's energy has tired me out, but my thoughts stray away from his college exploits to everything else happening here.

Steven's mom closing the door on me. Selena telling me not to go snooping around. How Noah Michaelson keeps coming by. And why I don't mind it so much.

A few minutes later, the front screen door opens and Caleb strides out with Ella on his heels. The hound's chocolate eyes light up when she sees me sprawled out on the steps and she immediately flops in my lap.

"Everything okay? With you and Jen . . . and Jay and all that?" Caleb doesn't beat around the bush.

"What do you think?"

"I think . . ." Caleb looks to the sky, searching for the right word. It's not there, apparently, because he turns back to me and shrugs. "I don't know. You tell me."

"I would if I knew." Ella raises her head with a whimper. "At least you still love me," I say pathetically, stroking her long, velvety ears.

"That's some epic feeling sorry for yourself, Kayla Koala," Caleb says, sitting next to me.

I lean back on the porch, soaking the last warmth of the wooden boards into my back and sigh. "I know. I make myself cringe."

Caleb brushes a handful of dead, crushed leaves from the lower step. "I can imagine it hasn't been easy since you've been back."

"For a while, I thought it was going to be okay," I say. "Jay said in front of everybody that it was an accident. Jen and Selena and I are friends again. But . . . things aren't so clear. I don't know what's real. Or right."

He sits with his back slightly hunched over and throws a stick for Ella. She bounds into the yard. "I know moving on's the whole reason you came back, but things don't always work out the way we want. Maybe it'd be better if you accepted, I don't know, that other people might not be ready to get past this the way you are."

It's more complicated than that is what I want to tell him. Instead I say, "That's what Noah says."

Caleb nudges me in the side. "Who's Noah? New flame for my baby sister?"

Heat flares in my shoulders and I look away. "He's not a new flame. He's— I don't know what he is. He's different."

"Wait. Do you mean Noah Michaelson up the road? I didn't know you two hung out. I think the last time I even talked to him was when you were in first or second grade. We used to barbecue with his family, remember? Then his mom took him to the Philippines for a year and we didn't see much of them anymore after that." Caleb leans back on his palms. "Yeah, he's different all right."

I narrow my eyes at him. "You don't mean because he's half Filipino."

He makes a sound. "*No.* I don't mean that. At least, that not why I think he's different. Except that *is* part of why he's different," he muses. "Hm. Other people . . ." He shrugs. "I don't know. He got quiet."

This time Ella brings the stick to me. I study it for a moment, looking at where the bark is discolored from her bites. Then I toss it into the yard. The porch shudders as she bounds off it. "He doesn't seem to care that I was the person driving the car that night. And that makes him different to me."

"Everyone else will come around. It was an accident."

"Maybe." I wipe my hands on my jeans and look over at him. "Tell me about school."

"It's a good school." He flashes me a mischievous look. "Lots of cute girls."

I snort. "That's eighty percent of what you're doing there, isn't it? A class here and there, I guess. To make Mom and Dad happy."

"Just a few," Caleb says.

"You're glad you went?"

"Sure. That's what we're supposed to do, right?"

"It's not what I want to do."

Caleb throws the stick then runs his palm over his hair. "There's a whole world outside this town, you know."

"I know. But this was always where I wanted to be. I know I'm supposed to be . . . I don't know . . . finding myself. My place in the world. Or something. But I've always known this was my place."

"There are worse places. But . . . what if there are better places, too?"

I sigh. I'm not stupid. I know there are all kinds of places out there. Things to like across the globe. But this is where I always want to come back home.

"Want to see something?" I ask.

"Is it gross?"

"You wish." I lead him to the boat, still propped up on two-by-fours but looking solid from the sand job. It makes me think of home, ties me to this town, somehow. Because I rebuilt it here. Because I imagine it drifting down this river.

Because I can see the people I've known and loved my whole life sitting in it.

Caleb whistles low. "Looks great, Kayla Koala."

I can't hide a huge grin because something good, hearing praise, feels like everything right now.

"Ella wants to go for a hike," Caleb announces, pushing into my room without knocking. I look up from my pillow to the window—still dark outside—and raise my eyebrows sleepily.

"It's the middle of the night, you psycho. Why are you awake?"

"It's four forty-five. Enough time to get out on the trail and get you back here in time for school. Supposed to be a bee-utiful day!"

Who is this guy with the chipper voice? I've never known Caleb to be up before lunch when he didn't have to be.

"Okay. Have fun. Take a picture of the beautiful day for me."

He puts his foot on Ella's rear end and nudges her into my room. She gazes up at me mournfully, like she doesn't really want to be awake, either. "She wants you to come along," he presses.

"Is that what she said? She doesn't look it."

"Yeah. 'Kaywa walk wif us.' Exactly like that."

"You're as dumb as she is, you know that?" But I'm already rolling out of bed and reaching for my shoes. Once awake, I can't fall back to sleep again. It's a curse.

"Actually, she is highly intelligent. She says don't get me and her mixed up. It's insulting."

Ella bounds into the back of Caleb's truck and he slams the rusty tailgate shut. We head out of town, filling the forty-five-minute drive with music and looking out at the scenery. The farther we get from our town's river boundary, the more open my lungs feel, the fresher the air.

We take the two-mile trail up to the bluff of Point Fellows; the path is well-worn after the summer season of hikers, and the last of the wildflowers scramble over one another on either side to reach highest and steal the most sun rays. Ella leaps into the flowers excitedly, nearly lost in the darkness, sniffing everything at a frantic pace before rejoining us on the trail with a wild bark and a coat full of petals and burrs.

At the top of the rock, Caleb pulls two bottles of water out of his backpack and we sit on the edge, our legs dangling over the valley below, and wait for sunrise. Ella flops on her side and settles into a nap. The landscape rolls gently, water and a sage-green pasture dotted with yellow and lavender flowers, shadowed by lingering early-morning darkness. I feel like a different person. Free.

"I love the view from up here," Caleb says.

"Me too."

"I miss it when I'm gone."

I would, too. I did, last summer. When real views were

replaced by endless stretches of little mowed lawns and too-bright night skies.

"I think there's something I should tell you," he continues. He tips back his head and finishes the last of his water, crushes the bottle, and stashes it back in his pack. "I wasn't going to but . . . being up here clears my mind, you know? Or maybe it just loosens my tongue because my mind . . ." He shakes his head and sighs. "You know Hailey."

I lean back on my hands. "Bean's sister. Obviously."

"Yeah. So, we were at this river party last year during spring break and people were pretty drunk. I was driving so . . ." He shrugs. "I wasn't. Drunk. I was hanging out with Joe Davis and Karl Schmidt and they were acting like total asses. Karl ended up practically drowning in the river."

"And?" Already, this conversation is tiring me out quicker than the hike and the thinner air up here combined. "I was at that party, remember?"

Caleb gives me a sharp look for interrupting. "I walked away from them, to be alone for a while. Headed over to the old storehouse up the way. You know the one. I don't know. Even though I'd gone to the party and was having a good time . . . I started feeling like I kind of wanted to think. That was the morning I'd heard about the Ozarks camp job and there was this weird moment at the party when I realized I was leaving home for good in just a couple of months. But the storehouse wasn't empty." He lifts a leg and wraps one arm around the knee. "Someone was in there. Crying. I almost turned around and walked away. Partly not to disturb them but partly because I didn't want to get involved in whatever drama was going on. There's always some kind of drama at those parties."

"Yeah," I say, wondering how much of what he's going to say has to do with our last conversation we had up here: the things we don't do even though we're supposed to.

"But she said my name. Hailey did. She got up and came over to me and . . . she was kind of messed up. Her hair was everywhere and her makeup was smeared and her clothes were all wet and muddy. She asked me to take her home. But not to her house. She was really . . . insistent about that. So I snuck her into our house and she took a shower and borrowed one of my T-shirts. She didn't want to talk about what had happened. She just said she and her boyfriend had gotten in a fight."

I squint at the horizon. The land is beautifully wild, edged in the distance with trees that give the view a shapely, finished feel, like eyebrows on a face.

"She was with Jay then," I say. "He'd dunked her in the river and she was pissed. Can't blame her. They broke up after that party. It wasn't a big deal. She was leaving anyway."

They were always up and down.

"I'm not saying anything bad happened between them. . . ."

I unscrew and screw the cap on the water bottle. Unscrew. Screw. Unscrew. "That's what it sounds like you're saying."

"Yeah, well, maybe I am, maybe I'm not. I don't actually know."

"Point is?"

He turns his narrow gaze from the valley to me and releases his leg again. "Point is, smart-ass, I brought you up here because I'm worried. Why were you in that car with Jay and Steven? Are you . . . okay?"

I take a long drink of water. What Caleb's hinting at makes my forearms itch. If he has something to say, he should just put it out there. In the open. Stop tripping around like a dog with a burr in its paw. It's not his style.

Because yes, I'm okay. And also . . . no, I don't know when I'll ever be okay again. But not because my ankle throbs sometimes or because the glint of Jay's eye against a black sky visits my nightmares or because I remember where the purple bruises bloomed on the inside of my bicep. It's because I know Bean's *not* okay. So, why isn't knowing that enough? Why isn't it bigger than my wanting to come home?

"Driving," I finally say, flatly. "That's why I was in the car."

Caleb gives me a long look before deciding my answer is enough. He takes my water from me and shoves it in a side pocket of his backpack.

We stand and brush the dirt off our shorts before turning

back toward the trail. A rough wind rushes through the grasses and draws goose bumps over my arms. I reach up and tighten my ponytail. A surprising rush of anger warms my neck.

"How come you didn't confront Jay? About Hailey?"

He plays with the strap hanging off the bottom of his backpack for a moment. "What do you mean?"

"We both know what I mean. Something bad happened between them. Everyone knows it but nobody says it. And you saw something. So why'd you let it go?"

"Everyone doesn't know it." But he pauses and somewhere in that pause we let truth take over. "She didn't want me to do anything. She didn't want anyone to know."

"How do *you* know that?" I say.

What I want from him is something solid, something that would help me know I did the right thing by keeping my secrets to myself when, right now, I'm certain it was the wrong thing. But Caleb can't give that to me. He doesn't know how to be the brave one any more than I do. I've always liked being close to my brother. Being like him. Except now, when it's as clear as the cloudless morning sky that we're both cowards.

"She never brought it up after that." His excuse is too much like mine. "I mean, she would have told someone if she wanted to deal with it that way, right?"

Not if it was her word against his. If she was worried what

people would do. How they would harass her family. She wouldn't say anything. As a survival tactic.

It's the route I took. The one Hailey took, the one Caleb took.

I think about the way Bean's looked at me since I've been back. The hope that fell from her eyes when I wouldn't confirm my memory of that night last summer.

It's been pinching at the back of my mind for a while . . . this sense that what I've thought was true isn't. The tenuous feeling of safety that came with keeping a secret I've argued wanted to be kept.

Even if, really, it wanted to be free.

I gnaw on the inside of my mouth for a moment, frustration building. He's worried about *me*. What about Hailey? What about Bean? What do we owe them? I rub the inside of my wrist and my voice sounds far away when I finally speak. "Is that the excuse you make when you struggle with whether you did the right thing? With whether you're a good person or not?"

Caleb takes a step back, his expression loosened slightly with shock. But I'm not sorry I said it. Only sorry how well I understand it.

SPRING

"NOAH MICHAELSON GRABBED ME after school and asked if he could bring some of his friends to the party," I announced as I brushed gloss across my lips. "I think guys he plays music with."

Jen paused with her mascara wand halfway to her lashes.

The big round bulbs in her bathroom made everything look so glamorous: the hot curlers in her hair, the way we sat on stools in our lacy bras and underwear, the array of makeup scattered over the bathroom counter. We were pinups.

She used the wand to separate two clumped-together lashes and shrugged. "As long as you told him we're not turning off the good music to listen to his banjo. We have enough beer to invite the whole town. Jay called Matt and Herman and got them to order a bunch of kegs." She closed the mascara cap and tossed it across the counter. "Those losers will do anything for him. Imagine staying here after graduation and just doing . . . nothing."

"Um, thanks?" I gave Jen a sideways look under the eyebrow pencil I held.

"I don't mean you." Her hair hung in a pile over one shoulder. She pulled it back and up, testing hairstyles, before letting it fall against her spine. "I just mean . . . Honestly, I'll be so glad when we get out of here and there's half a country between me and my brother."

I dropped the pencil, wiped off with a tissue the dark red lipstick I was wearing, and tried again with a glossy, soft pink color. "Why are you so mad at Jay today?"

"When am I not?" She laughed.

I scooted closer to her and wrapped my arms around her shoulders. We stared at ourselves, cuddled up, in the mirror, her narrow cheeks and pointed chin and slender arms and my rosy cheeks and square chin and arms round with muscles.

"School's out, Jen. Be happy! Jay's just . . . Jay. A little bit annoying, but what brother isn't? Remember when he stayed up all night helping you fill out valentines for the entire junior class last February? And how he always washes your car when he washes his?"

Her mouth twitched. "He sometimes does good things. True. But I don't think . . ." Jen swallowed and brought her hands to rest on my forearm. In the mirror, her eyes changed. Losing their fight and softening into something like panic. The faucet dripped twice before she spoke again.

She spoke quietly, as if her voice would shatter the mirror if she was too loud. "I think sometimes about how nice it will be to be my own person. Not Jay's twin or one of the

Brewsters. No one to tell me what to do or not to do . . ."
Her laugh was so soft it almost didn't exist. "That sounds so
dramatic, right? I'm just looking forward to getting to choose
who to have in my life."

"I hope you'll choose me." I squeezed her shoulders.

The set of Jen's mouth was beginning to worry me. Or
maybe it wasn't that. Not something physical I could see,
but there was a tremor in the air, a feeling that her emotions
had become blurry and pixelated. Confused. And hidden
from me.

Something had happened and she didn't want me to
know about it.

"Kayla, I will *always* choose you. I can't imagine going
to college without you. You'll be my reminder of everything
good about home when I get homesick. I wish you would just
come with me."

"I'll just have to send you pie when you get depressed at
college." I straightened up again and reached for the gold
liquid eyeliner. She hated that I didn't want to go with her.
And her hate made me feel wrong.

"You make the best pie. See? That's exactly what I mean.
Any time I feel down, you're there with pie or you get my
butt on a horse or you just . . . are *you*. And that's what I'm
going to need. But you won't be there. You're my favorite,
you know?"

I nodded airily and pulled the gold along my lower

eyelash line. "How could I not be?"

She giggled, and in a moment, the fragile mood that had settled over the bathroom dissipated like a cloud of shower steam out the window.

FALL

THE CLOUDS ARE GRAY with unshed rain as I wait for the school bus Thursday morning. I pull my hood up. I half expect Noah to come roaring by, tossing rust flakes off the side of his truck. But then I shrink at the idea that I'm getting used to him showing up when I most want him to. Or least expect him to. I don't know how different those things are. If there are any differences.

When I step off the bus at school, the skies open. I scan the students picking up speed to get into the school before they're drenched. Just ahead of me, Bean tucks her hair behind her ear then brushes the back of her hand across her cheek. She's not walking quickly. I'm not walking at all. My hoodie isn't doing much of a job keeping out the rain. Neither are my shoes. Water trickles down the back of my neck and soaks into my socks.

I sprint across the lawn to catch Bean before she enters the school, knowing conversations like this are easier outside where fewer people are paying attention, where words disappear into the wind whipping our bags and clothes, blowing someone's homework into the parking lot.

But before I can catch her, she mounts the one step and disappears into the building. It's five minutes before first bell and the hallways are crowded. My shoes squeak. I stick close to Bean, falling into step behind her. She stops abruptly at her locker and I bump into her.

"We were close," I blurt out. "What happened?" She hasn't turned around, so she misses the way I cringe at my words and sink back into myself until I feel my heels scrape the backs of my shoes. What a stupid thing to say when I, too, have been avoiding Bean. To confront her about friendships when I've managed ours so poorly makes me a hypocrite.

What I really mean to say is *You never told the police. Never filed a report. Dumping old friends is suspicious. Changing our patterns, acting out of turn . . . all those things that are supposed to clue people in that something is wrong. And since no one's picked up on that or they're ignoring that or . . . something . . . that means that not telling is what we've decided, right? To go along like nothing happened? Right?* Right?

She spins the lock open and faces me. The redness around her eyes gives her away and my heart shrinks. It wasn't the rain she was wiping away. "Nothing. We're fine."

"We're not," I say softly. "Not you and me. Not . . . any of us."

There's an ache growing in my chest. Slow to spark, steady in building, then, suddenly, roaring. Painful, licking flame.

We were four. We were four in one town with one winding river and a diner with sweet rolls the size of our heads. We *were*.

Her eyes start to flicker: to the left, over my shoulder, toward the entry doors.

The wind howls through, keeping the doors open without anyone holding them, and I realize that in my longing for Jen's friendship again and my desperation to put that night last May out of my thoughts, that I've neglected one of the four. The one who needs me the most. The one I need the most.

"Maybe we could do something next . . ." I trail off as her eyes lock on something behind me.

I already know who I'll see standing there when I turn around, but I do it anyway to see Jen watching us with a blank expression, and when I catch her eye, I can't read anything there. Selena is next to her, looking suspicious. It's that moment I stop caring, though. What Selena might think. Whether or not Jen would approve of my snooping. There's something about realizing how cowardly Caleb and I have been that's lit the tiniest flame of courage inside me. That makes me believe I can fight to keep all of my friends.

I look at Bean again. "I came home, but so much changed while I was gone, Bean."

"People change. It happens." Bean tugs on a curl lying over her shoulder. She looks away from Jen and Selena and stares at the contents of her locker for a moment. I'm waiting for her to give me some indication that we can close the door on the past and move forward.

And when she finally looks back at me, maybe she sees

what I want. Maybe she doesn't want to give me that. She says, "You shouldn't be asking about why."

I want to ask her why not but I don't. I just say, "That's what Selena said."

I see Bean's disappointment in a sudden twisting of her mouth.

But it should be worse. It should be a loud, angry scream or a cry of pain.

Bean's best friend in the world knows what happened but turned her back on Bean anyway. And yet. Bean blinks slowly, smooths the frown from her face, drops the curl around her finger, and says, "She's right, I guess. See you, Kayla."

Bean moves down the hall and around the corner, forgetting to close her locker. I shut it and turn the dial slowly. Last year, we all knew each other's codes.

When I turn back around, Jen's walked away, but Selena still stands there, has walked closer and is watching me, chewing on the eraser end of a pencil.

"Selena," I begin. I have nothing to follow her name with.

She cocks her head to the side. "Kayla," she says, "I told you not to snoop."

Then she turns away and I'm standing here alone, again.

I call Bean and leave a message when she doesn't answer.

"It's me . . . ," I begin.

But that doesn't feel right. Like I am beyond recognition.

I start again. "It's Kayla. I thought we could go to the home-coming dance together. Want to be my date? Call me back."

She never calls.

I believed Selena when she said Bean was the one to walk away from her friends. I would have understood why, in those first days after the accident. Now, I don't know what's going through Bean's head. Why and how she can exist, calmly, day to day, beside these people when the anger inside me feels too heavy to move, but inside her . . . it should be ferocious and explosive. Because Bean had wanted to tell—she *did* tell someone, her best friend. Bean hasn't stayed silent because she's wanted to. It's because she's had to.

I could have changed that. I still *can* change that.

Except for the fear. The fear that might be, after all, big-ger than the anger I feel.

In a town that felt, for so long and in the best way pos-sible, like nothing ever changes, things have. They changed that night and they changed while I was gone and I can't change them back to the way they were before I left. Even though I keep trying.

I don't want to be angry and I don't want to be afraid. Not of my own home.

I lie in the boat and drink orange soda, waiting for Jen to come pick me up for the homecoming carnival. After the storm passed, the sky became clear and sunshiny again.

I text Noah. *Are you going to the carnival?*

Who is this? he texts back. Then, *Just kidding. Probably going.*

Yesterday, at school, I caught Noah's eye as we walked in opposite directions down the hallway. My breathing picked up as he came nearer to me. His washed-out orange T-shirt was printed with a cartoon moose. It stretched nicely across his shoulders. I stopped walking, preparing to say something to him, but Jen grabbed my wrist to pull me along. So Noah and I passed each other wordlessly. But I could see the question in his eyes. His wondering if, since I have my old friends back, he is out of the picture.

Out of my life.

I don't want him to be.

I want him and everyone else. That's why I came back. That's what I've worked for.

And I want Bean back, too. So why does she stay away from me—as though we hadn't both decided to keep our secrets? As though we aren't *both* pretending nothing's wrong?

Maybe I'm only trying to convince myself that we're pretending. Maybe the world would split in half if Bean knew I remembered everything from that night.

Of course she's not friends with Jen and Selena anymore. Or me.

How can she even look at us without feeling ill?

I am so still that I feel the earth spinning under me. A

wave of dizziness blackens my vision. I sit up and lean over the edge of the boat so that my orange puke hits the grass instead of my boat.

Just when back-to-school month is winding down, the events pick up with a fever: the carnival tonight, dance tomorrow night, and then, finally, the big game Saturday against Highland Hills, the crappiest team in the state. Homecoming is always scheduled when the team with the worst record the previous season comes to Winbrooke. A guaranteed win keeps the alumni who travel back home once a year feeling like it was worth their time.

I zip up a hoodie to ward off the cool breeze running across the school courtyard at the carnival. It smells good. Everything. The lingering dampness and the air heavy with earth and food booths and the bales of hay used as seating.

"The lineup for the kissing booth sucks," Selena says as she and I wait for Jen to finish her shift in the dunk tank. "Why even bother?"

I shrug and examine the pink-and-orange hedgehog-looking stuffed animal I won at the balloon race in Game Alley. I've always been good at fair games. Its eyes are crooked, but I like the imperfection.

"Kissing booths are gross. All that germ swapping. Ick."

Selena raises an eyebrow at me. "I guess it's a good thing I only date college guys, then."

"Right, because *they're* known for keeping their germs to themselves."

"Does your brother keep his germs to himself?" Her eyes flick over my shoulder. "I forgot how cute he is."

I turn my head and see Caleb trying to flip rubber frogs onto lily pads floating in a kiddie pool of water. Eric, who I've seen a couple of times at my house since Caleb came home, is standing next to him with that hero-worshipping expression he always uses when he looks at my brother. But Caleb is a lackluster hero. He misses the lily pad every time, passes over more money, and keeps missing, whooping and hollering it up each time a frog lands in the water, just like the old Caleb would. He's starting to gather a crowd.

"What happened to Dan?" I ask.

"I'm not known for keeping my germs to myself, either." Her smile is pure naughty girl.

I roll my eyes and drag Selena toward the food booths. "I'm hungry. Corn dogs, root beer, and funnel cakes or death!"

"You mean corn dogs, root beer, funnel cakes, *and* death." She giggles, holding her belly.

"You think *that's* bad? Your cute Caleb always gets deep-fried Ding Dongs."

Her sound of disgust is accentuated by the roar of the crowd as Caleb, finally, lands a lily pad.

We walk up and down the booths and, food in hand,

enter the football stadium and climb the bleachers until we're happy with our view. A farmer in a baseball cap sips punch from a red plastic cup a couple of rows down. Some freshman boys from school balance on the railing at the very top of the bleachers, showing off for their girlfriends sitting below them. A few guys on the football team toss the ball around below us. The breeze plays with my ponytail. Point Fellows is a blur in the distance.

I breathe in and out slowly.

Selena's mouth is full of funnel cake.

I take a huge bite of corn dog and mustard. When I swallow, I set my plate on the seat next to me. "Jay was drunk that night."

Selena brushes her hands together and a wispy cloud of powdered sugar blows toward the stadium floor.

"At least that," she finally says.

"So how come that didn't come out in the accident report?"

A length of hair twists around her finger slowly. "His mom's Erica Brewster. She could've made people think Steven was the one driving the car if she'd wanted to. But does it matter? Jay wasn't driving. Nothing against the law about being drunk in the passenger seat."

I squirm at the mention of Jay's mom. Even now, she avoids looking at me when I'm at the Brewsters' house.

"Except for that whole underage thing."

Selena laugh-coughs. "Like anyone cares."

Jen pokes her head into the stadium, rubbing a towel over wet hair, and waves us over.

"Jen's done with the dunk tank," I say. And then, "I think his being drunk matters. In a different way."

"Fuck, Kayla. Boys get drunk all the time."

It's just what boys do.

She shouldn't have been drinking. She shouldn't have walked off alone. She shouldn't have flirted with him. She shouldn't have worn that skirt.

A strain of music from several bleachers over catches my attention. A small group surrounds a boy playing a guitar. Not Noah. But suddenly, I want to find him. I scan the crowd and, after a moment, spot his wet-sand hair at the dart throw booth. He pulls his arm back and sends a dart flying. I hear a balloon pop. Or maybe I imagine the sound.

I will him to turn around and look at me. He doesn't.

"You should ask someone to the dance," Selena says.

I did.

"No, it's too late for that," I say.

I wonder who Noah is going with. If he's going. I wonder what he'd say if I asked him. The way he'd have to stammer out a no, trying not to hurt my feelings, because why would he want to go with a girl who seems to have ditched him at the first sign of her old friends?

I flick a mosquito off the edge of my plate. "Let's go. Jen's waiting for us."

We head back down, tossing our half-eaten food in the garbage, and reenter the mix of students, faculty, and alumni on the field.

"Was the water cold?" I ask Jen.

"Freezing." Jen shudders and wraps her towel tighter around her shoulders. "Have you seen Jay?"

"I don't think he's here yet," Selena says.

"Yeah, too much to expect he'd take a turn at the dunk tank." Jen grimaces. A halfhearted attempt to pretend she is teasing. "Jerk."

At a souvenir booth, Bean and her new friend Grace perform a mock fight with foam gladiator swords. My feet still; I watch them for a long time. Too long.

Grace looks up at me and her mouth twists with a sheepish smile. To catch her acting like a kid.

But when Bean sees me her face loses its smile. She presses her lips into a thin line and sticks the sword back in the vendor's basket.

"Hurry up, Kayla," Jen calls, and I follow her, pretending that I haven't been looking at Bean. I don't think she's noticed and then it doesn't matter because everyone starts cheering.

"Yeah, man, there he is!" someone yells next to me,

clapping his hands above his head. The whistle he gives is shrill and hurts my ears.

Jay Brewster has finally decided to grace us all with his presence.

We get ready for the homecoming dance at Jen's house because she has a date to come pick her up and I'm just riding along in the backseat.

Maybe I *should* have asked Noah to come with me.

Maybe I shouldn't be going at all.

Jen's white strapless dress hugs her body, beginning where her small breasts start to squish out at the top and ending halfway up her thigh. Her legs are long, long, long. She leaves her hair loose and does her face in mod makeup: thick black eyeliner on her top lid and nude lipstick. My dress is black with a full, but short, tulle skirt. I pull my hair back into a bun and fill my lips with deep red lipstick. We teeter around Jen's room in our sky-high heels; I'm a little better at walking in mine than Jen, despite my ankle. Her date rings the doorbell as I'm pulling on my lace gloves.

Erica Brewster pokes her head in.

"T. J. is here," she says to Jen. Always to Jen, even when I'm standing next to her. Never saying something to me, looking at me, thinking about me.

"My mom's a bitch," Jen always says, even if I don't bring it up. "Ignore her."

I do ignore her, and Erica ignores me back, and that, I know, is as good as it will ever get with her.

Downstairs, T. J. stands in the entryway with Jay. They're both wearing black dress pants, but T. J. has a gray vest over a pink dress shirt while Jay's wearing a tie and jacket. A few months ago, I would have gotten mad at Jen for not asking if it was okay for her and T. J. to go to the dance together. T. J. had been *my* crush. But now, I hear him say, "Hey, Kayla," and my name sounds a little bit like "killa" still, and I don't care that Jen didn't ask me if it's okay to go with him.

I'm not the same Kayla.

Jay says hi, too, and not for the first time, I wonder, *How can he look at me when last summer I drove into a ditch to escape him?* How can our interaction right now be so normal? As though Jay doesn't care what he's done, what I've done, what I might know about him?

He has never had to care.

T. J. looks up at Jen with the smile of a boy who knows he's getting lucky later on. Jay slaps him on the back, says, "Keep it clean, kids," like Jen isn't the older twin by five minutes, and heads out the door, his keys in hand, to meet up with his own date.

"Shall we?" T. J. holds his arm out toward Jen. I look away from his white-knight performance and fall in line somewhere behind the two of them and their nervous laughter.

The high school gym is decorated like every high school

gym in every teen movie's dance scene. Balloon towers flank the doors; there are food tables and a picture-arch thing. Long streamers crisscross over our heads. And there's a DJ on the stage under a rainbow of strobe lights. By the time we arrive, couples are slow-dancing badly to an administration-approved soundtrack.

I look around for Bean.

Then force myself not to look around for Bean.

Jen and Selena ditch their dates for three songs in a row so we girls can dance in a little circle. We let a few others in—the other homecoming princesses, a friend or two—but not everyone. In between songs, I look out and think how, with another decision, those people might have been me.

Halfway through the night, I allow myself to recognize that Bean isn't here. Then the main lights come on and the homecoming court is introduced, one by one. There are jokes about a brother and sister winning king and queen, but I guess the jokes aren't wrong because, sure enough, it's Jay and Jen standing on that stage with crowns on their heads when all is said and done.

It's the culminating moment they both have waited on for years. In another life, it could have been me up there with Jay. Or Bean. Always, though, it would have been Jay.

Instead of dancing with each other, like the king and queen normally do, Jen and Jay each grab their dates and take the floor.

I smile for Jen because the spotlight lifts the gold tones in her hair and her dress flashes and T. J. smiles like he's the luckiest guy in the room. The moment passes when Maria and Jay, slowly spinning in a circle, block my view of Jen. I shiver. Someone has opened the doors to let out some of the sweaty stink of a bunch of teenagers packed into one room and it's suddenly so cold. My jaw muscles clench. Selena and her home-from-college date head out onto the dance floor when the DJ announces it's open to everyone, and I'm left standing here alone.

I walk outside and call my mom to ask her to come get me. I know she's surprised by the way a too-long silence answers my request for a ride. But then she simply says she's on her way and I'm grateful that she sees some things clearly but not other things. I let the heels of my shoes sink into the grass.

"The party's inside," Noah says, coming up behind me.

"Then why aren't you in there?" I turn to look at him. His button-down shirt is open at the collar and he's wearing skate shoes with his khaki pants. Shivers erupt over my bare shoulders, but they have nothing to do with the cold. "Who are you here with?"

"No one. I just got off work."

"And you came here instead of anywhere else?"

He doesn't answer. A roar of laughter comes from the open gym doors, but I don't see who's making the noise or what they've done that's so funny because I'm watching Noah watch me. My ribs feel like a cage for a panicked bird. His gaze travels over my bare collarbone but no more before returning to my chin, my lips, my eyes. Boldness and timidity battle in me until I catch a breath at the way he swallows nervously and then I make a decision.

I square my body to his and take his hand in mine before I can stop myself. Think better of it. Let my arm settle on his shoulder and then, when his goes around my waist, curve mine around his neck. He knows how to keep rhythm and so we shuffle in time to the song drifting over to us, my heels crushing grass, his shoes sliding over dirt.

"You came here instead of anywhere else," he says into my hair. Somehow I know he's not talking about the dance.

Headlights brighten the night and I pull away from Noah. My body is not happy. It wants to stay in that embrace, under that warm, searching gaze.

But I open my mom's car door and get in.

"Thanks for picking me up," I tell her.

"Is that Noah Michaelson?" she asks, peering out my window as we pull away.

Noah waits, hands in his pockets, until we're out of sight.

"Yeah." I prop my elbow against the door and rest the side of my head in my hand. "That's Noah."

When we pull into our driveway, I say, "I'm pretty tired. Going to head to bed."

I'm halfway up the stairs when she says my name. I look down at her, standing in the entryway with the car keys held in her fist. She isn't wearing her gardening hat anymore like she was before I left for Jen's house earlier in the day, but her hair is still flattened against her head. It's not the sort of thing she worries about.

She worries about me.

It takes her a few moments to decide what to say to me. I guess at the possibilities but there are so many I lose track. In the end, she only says, "Good night."

"Night, Mom."

I wait until I hear her and Dad's low voices talking in the kitchen before climbing the rest of the stairs. I replay Noah's face and words in my mind with each step I take. Yes, I came back here. I came back to reclaim a world of love and laughter, a place with sprinkles of magic at the edges. But the people who used to live there aren't the same. The dust in the air at sunrise doesn't shimmer anymore; it just looks dirty. The river smells murky instead of fresh. The magic is gone. From this place . . . and from me.

And what do I do about that? I walk into my room. For a moment, facing my closed closet door, I wish I had asked Mom to come up with me. To face this excavation together. To tell me what to do.

I open the closet door. Pull out the bag from the hospital. The bag from that night. Everything inside is folded neatly.

There's a form on top with my name on it. It's obvious no one has gone through this bag until now. And I get that—the desire to be distanced from that night. These things are better left in the back of the closet, forgotten.

No. They're not.

I scratch my shoulder absently, gathering strength. Then I reach in. Feel the remnants of that night. Silky black shorts. The hardness of a high heel.

The paramedics would have assumed every item on me was mine. My clothing. My shoes. Whatever was in my pocket.

What about what wasn't on me? My purse. My driver's license.

I pause with my hands buried in purple sequins.

Why did no one say anything about me not having my license?

The heat on my face is like sticking my head too far into an oven. I get up, leaving the bag on the floor, and splash my face with cold water in the bathroom sink.

I go back to my room.

This time I pull everything out. Fling out the clothing piece by piece. The heels thump against the wall. And, at the bottom, is a memory.

A phone.

I walk away from it again. Then back to it. Pick it up and cradle it in my palm. It's not my phone. It's Steven's. Just

something else thrown from the car that night. Like Steven.
Like me.

I'd tucked it in my pocket, that night last spring.

And made a promise to Bean.

SPRING

SELENA AND BEAN SHOWED up in a cloud of perfume and flowing dresses an hour before the party started, just as Jen and I were starting to get dressed.

"When do your parents leave?" Selena checked her hair in the bathroom and added a spritz of hairspray to an errant flyaway.

"Any minute," Jen said.

As if she knew we were talking about her, Erica Brewster poked her head in Jen's room and tapped her red fingernails against the doorframe. "We're going," she said. Her eyes swept over me and Jen and Bean. "You girls look so nice."

"Hi, Mrs. Brewster," Selena yelled from the bathroom.

"You look nice, too, Selena," Jen's mom called across the room, even though she couldn't see Selena. "Have a good night and be good. I have my cell so call if you need me. Kayla, I'm sure you'll keep everyone out of trouble." Her smile reached the corners of her eyes. "I know I can trust you for that."

"I will do my best." I waved as she faded out of sight down the hall.

Jen turned to me, her eyes sparkly. "Alone. Finally."

The four of us grinned and a shiver of anticipation bolted up my spine. I reached for Jen's music and clicked it on, turning on the balls of my feet to the thump of bass.

In the bathroom, Selena exchanged the hairspray for the bottle of vodka and cranberry juice she'd stashed in her bag and began passing it around. The juice mix was warm and I declined.

"Orange juice next time," I said. "That cranberry stuff you get is basically red sugar water."

"Lighten up, Kayla," Selena said. She lifted an eyebrow at me over the lip of the bottle.

"I'll wait for something better."

"Don't we all," Jen said.

Jay came home, bringing a handful of noisy guys with him, and we watched them set up the kegs in the backyard and pull the cover off the hot tub. Jen told them where to sink tiki torches into the grass and set tables up on the wood deck off the back of the house. Bean and I emptied bags of chips into big plastic bowls.

"You're missing the bowl," I said as half of the pretzels Bean was pouring ended up on the table.

"Oops." She giggled and moved her whole body to see the mess she was making. Her feet stumbled over each other and I laughed and put a hand to her shoulder to keep her steady.

"How much booze has Selena given you?" Bean and I

were the nondrinkers, usually. The lightweights.

"Oh God, I don't know. We had some at my house before we came over." She stopped, her eyes lifted to some point over my head, and pointed. "Look at that."

I turned and together we watched the gold and scarlet brushstrokes of the sunset deepen and bleed into one another. Across the table, Bean's hand found mine. We breathed out the air of day and in the air of the falling night. "You should paint it."

"It's beautiful," she said softly. Her pale face reflected the dying yellow rays of the sun, her eyes took on a washed-out turquoise color that reminded me of the waves that lapped against the shore during our Florida spring break vacation. I squeezed her hand.

"Now kiss."

The moment was broken by a grating boy voice behind us. We turned.

Steven McInnis pointed his phone at us, his arm steady, his eyes fixed on the screen. Bean frowned.

"We're not here for you to get your rocks off." I swiped at his hand, but he whipped it away too quickly.

"Too bad. I could get into this thing."

"Piss off, Steven."

Steven shook his head. "Don't be like that, Kayla. Why do you have to be cruel? *Smile.* It's the first day of summer. You look prettier that way."

I rolled my eyes at him. "I'm not trying to look pretty for you."

Walking up behind him, Selena pulled her fist back and slammed it into Steven's shoulder.

His face crumpled. "What the hell . . ."

"Stop being an asshole, asshole."

Steven flashed her a look, all dark eyebrows and shaded eyes, but skulked off to bug someone else.

I flashed Selena a grateful smile. "I'm going to run in the house and grab Bean some water," I said. "You should stay with her. She might need . . . holding up."

Bean stuck her tongue out at me and Selena laughed and slipped her arm through Bean's.

Through the window above the kitchen sink, I saw Steven do a dorky dance toward Maria. She planted her fists on her hips and ignored him. But the girl she was talking to giggled at him.

I took a drink of Bean's water. The yard was filling quickly as carloads of people emptied onto the Brewsters' sprawling green lawn. Someone turned the music up.

Jen caught sight of me and beckoned. I laughed at her come-hither expression and started to dance out to her.

I left the cup next to the sink. I forgot my worry for Bean in the house.

FALL

MY BIKE STILL CREAKS. It always will, I guess.

The phone burns a hole in my pocket.

My route takes me from one end of Third Street to the other, but it's too late—or too early—for the smell of baking rolls to sweeten my journey.

At Jen's house I stop and wait, staring at the dark windows, knowing she's still at the dance or in the backseat of the car I rode in earlier, parked down by the river or on a dark road somewhere. My house is an old farmhouse that my grandparents built when they moved out here ages and ages ago. Jen's house is brand-new. Shaped like a box with lots of windows. It's been here long enough that I don't think twice about it anymore, but when it was first built, I had to squint when I looked at it. It's like a boulder in the middle of the river, disturbing the natural flow of things.

It doesn't belong here.

I walk my bike another hundred yards or so before getting on again. It's easy to find the right spot. I look for signs: the bark ripped from a tree, the hill cresting just ahead. It lives in my head like a landscape painting I just found in the attic. Cloudy for all the dust I've blown off it but recognizable.

When I get there, I drop my bike and sit. I could be sitting on old oil or blood from the accident. It doesn't feel weird, and it doesn't feel familiar, like everything else in this town does. It feels like it shouldn't exist at all.

But I pull out the phone. I'd left it for an hour on the charger I found in Caleb's room. There are voices in my head telling me what I should and shouldn't do. Some belong to other people.

Don't go snooping.

You really don't remember anything about that night?

It's okay, it was an accident.

We already sold your pie.

Others are only mine.

Watch it.

Don't watch it. It will change everything.

It doesn't have to. Watch it.

Don't watch it, Kayla. Don't.

This phone belongs to a dead boy. I swipe my thumb across the face of it and blink as Steven's home screen loads. I'm glad it's not locked. Aren't I?

I choose the photo gallery from his apps and, before I lose my nerve, press on the first image that pops up. The video begins with the sound of clinking glass, of sloshing liquid. Of laughter and catcalls and faces pressed close to the screen. Big eyes, open mouths, dizzying camera movement. Then there's moving grass for a long time. A beer bottle falls to the ground.

A voice: "I just fucked up my shoes. You owe me a new pair."

"Like fuck I do."

"It's your house. Claim it on your insurance."

Guffaws.

My hands squeeze the phone so hard that it makes indentations in my skin.

There is a quick change of scenery. Jen's barn appears. Then grass again. Then the barn. I feel sick. Dig my heels into gravel and round my back so my head is closer to the ground. When I breathe, it smells like beer and horses. Someone left a stuffed animal here for Steven.

"Look who's out here," the familiar voice in the video says softly.

I stop watching because I have to.

I only listen, and listening is enough.

The conversation they almost have, because Bean's words are too slow and slurred to be a real conversation. Laughter. The argument over whether to turn off the video or not. More laughter.

Crying. And laughter. And suggestions so horrible I am sick again.

Another voice. I sit up. I hate hearing my recorded voice.

"Bean? Oh my God."

I flip the phone over again so the screen faces me. Just in

time to see a blur, someone say, "Shit," and watch it click off.

Another light fills my vision. I scoot farther back from the road, squinting into headlights. I can't tell whose car has pulled off the road in front of me until the lights go out and I recognize Bean's Honda. The driver's door opens.

"I come here sometimes, too," Bean says by way of a greeting as she steps out of her car. Her teal sequins glitter in the bath of her headlights. A pile of red hair sits on top of her head. Gravel crunches under her silver shoes.

The phone slips from my hands and lands under my leg.

"What are you doing here?" I ask.

"You asked me to be your homecoming date," she says. "I accept."

I've already changed out of my dress and into jeans.

"That's . . . kind of creepy, Bean."

"What is? You asking? Or me not calling to say yes before just showing up?"

"Showing up *here*."

"I wasn't planning on coming here. I was on my way to the dance. You rode right past me on Third and didn't even notice."

"And you followed." I can't decide if I wish I stayed at the dance now or if I'm glad Bean and I weren't seen together there. What I do know is that the way she's looking at me— intense, knowing, vindicated—scares me a little. I'm like an animal flushed from its burrow. No more hiding.

"I was curious where you were going. This is a strange choice for your after-party."

"It wasn't much of a party." I wince. I know we're not going to talk about the homecoming dance, but I want to. Anything to keep Bean from saying the things I'm certain she wants to say.

I can't stop her, though. All the words she's kept inside come tumbling out.

"I marked the tree so I'd remember where it happened." Bean points to the X dug into the bark behind me then to the furry fabric on the ground. "I brought that bear for the memorial. Does that seem sick to you?"

Yes, I want to say. But I can't. I don't want to think about Bean standing here, holding a gift for Steven's memorial because no one would listen to her.

"When I come back here, I think about how he died in the accident. Everyone says I'm the nicest girl they know, but I'm *glad* someone died. I wished someone else dead, too." She sits close to me and peers into my face, as though searching for something. Agreement. Confirmation. Because I, of all people, can't think poorly of her for wishing someone dead. And what she finds satisfies her because she nods. "I don't feel guilty, either, wishing that. Then I wouldn't have to look at him every day in school. And feel, over and over, what he did to me.

"It's what you wanted, too, huh, Kayla? For them to die.

Or to hurt them, somehow. *To not let them get away with it.* You did it on purpose. Turning the car into the ditch. You did that for me."

"I didn't . . . ," I croak. Swallow. "I didn't see everything. That night, I mean."

Her hand reaches out. Touches my shoulder. Pulls away. "Doesn't matter. You saw enough. You replay it. In your head." She nods at the phone. "With the video. You remember what happened now, don't you?"

I remember. I remembered long before "now." I didn't remember, yet, when they'd asked me, the police, so it wasn't a lie then. But I remembered long before I came home, the pieces falling into place as I explored Aunt Bea's suburban neighborhood in Kansas City. I remembered when I ate, the swallowing harder the more I thought. When I slept, my dreams taking on the graininess of an old movie, until the only thing I recognized was a night outlined in fear.

But every day I was gone, I talked to my parents. And when they didn't bring up what happened that night before the accident—the things that had led up to the accident—I realized that Bean hadn't told anyone what they did to her. And Bean's silence made me feel like I could come back. I thought she didn't *want* to tell. Eventually, I thought that maybe I had remembered things wrong. That it was all a mistake.

Jay was a star athlete. A hero. A boy everyone had such hope in. He could have any girl. And he certainly wouldn't have to rape someone.

I know better now. Rape isn't about sex.

"Does Jen know?" I ask softly.

"Yeah. She knows." Her expression softens. She swallows and looks at her keys cradled in her hands. "I told her that night. Before we heard about the accident. She told me I was drunk and hallucinating and that I should go home."

"I tried to come back for you," I say. "It would have been different." The moon glints off the silver key. Off sequins. Her skin is so pale. Why did I try so hard to come back for Bean that night but not after? How did her experience, how much I care about her, change so much in the time between the car crash and waking up? How can I still hesitate when she's right here, in front of me, putting so much faith in me?

"I know you did. Someone else gave me a ride home. I can't even remember who. The whole night was happening in a dream . . . a nightmare. I didn't hear about the accident until the next morning. I was in my room all night, staring at the wall like I'd lost my mind."

The same way I did all summer long. Eyes locked on the plain, white ceiling in Aunt Bea's guest room, seeing my memories as though they were being replayed in a rearview mirror.

"I needed to file a report, but how could I? Jen didn't believe me. If she didn't, who would?" She blinked. Her dark mascara made her green eyes pop. "You, of course. But then I learned you couldn't remember what happened. I was so worried about you. When I heard about the crash. After."

"Nothing to worry about," I mumble, because I never wanted her to waste her worry on me. I'd never deserved it.

She gives me a tiny smile. "When you came home, I thought it was because you'd remembered. I was hopeful for the first time in months. But even when you said you didn't remember . . . I knew the memories were there, in your head, somewhere. That's why I left that note in your locker the first week of school. I thought maybe it would trigger you or something."

"You didn't need me to remember," I say. "Your word—"

"What Jay did to Hailey . . . she left town earlier than she'd planned to. To stay safe. Because she knew if she stayed . . . if she told anyone . . ." Bean straightens up, lifts her chin to look at the sky. Her voice goes up a measure with incredulity, with impatience, with the unfairness of everything girls go through. "That's how it always goes, right? 'She shouldn't have been at that party. Shouldn't have been drinking. Shouldn't have worn a dress. He *was* her boyfriend, so of course it was a misunderstanding.'" She shakes her head and makes a low noise. "And it's Jay Brewster, so."

I know what she means. The Brewsters' house is new.

Doesn't really belong here. But the family does. Erica's influence as county prosecutor is nothing compared to Jen's uncle in the state senate.

But all that? Pales in comparison to the backing of a town that loves its golden boy.

"I didn't even know about what had happened between Hailey and Jay until days later. She could tell something was wrong, so I told her. She warned me. Don't tell anyone, she said. They will destroy us."

"Oh, Bean," I whisper.

Her eyes flick to me. "Yes, you understand that. The danger of telling. Hailey didn't tell because she was worried they would take it out on the rest of our family. They did anyway." Her laugh comes out as a strangled sob. "I don't even think it was ever about me. As a person. I think . . . I was just a part of this crazy power struggle with my sister. Because Hailey broke up with him."

I bury my face in my hands. Bean's probably right. How dare Hailey leave him? Boys like him think they're entitled to everything they want.

Bean sighs. "Hailey hates herself for that. But at least she's gone. And I had to stay here and *look* at him. I sit as far from him in classes as I can. I walk the other way when I see him in the hallways. But still, he's there." She slams her hand into the ground. "Every." Slam. "Day." Slam. "Knowing he would bury me if I told. Knowing I'd waited too long for . . .

the evidence. To be able to go to a doctor and say, 'Look at my body. Look what they did to it.'"

I brush the back of my wrist under my nose. Tamp down a shudder.

"It will kill my parents to know, Kayla," she says. "But this is destroying me. What they did. That he could do it again."

I clear my throat but my voice is still husky. I need to cough or scream or something loud, too loud. "I'm so sorry about Hailey."

"I know. I am, too. I'm sorry it happened and I'm sorry she couldn't tell. *Me*, at least. So I'd have been warned." She kicks a row of gravel and crouches in front of me. Tears stream down her face. "But I know how dangerous it is to let someone like him off the hook. And now you know. Now there's a witness and they're going to pay for what they did. It won't ever. Happen. Again."

"I didn't see everything," I repeat feebly, because my head is filled with buzzing and I can't think of what else to say. How to agree with her but . . . how to explain why I came home, after all. How telling the truth destroys everything that I've been working for and how I can't, not yet, think about losing my home forever.

How I really wish that accident *had* stolen the memory of that night from me. I'd give anything not to have to choose.

"That's okay," she whispers. "You know, anyway. You

won't let them get away with it. Especially with the way they'd grabbed you. I remember that. The things they must have said to you . . . You won't let them get away with that. I know you won't. Because you drove the car into the ditch. On purpose. That means something. And once you tell Jen . . . she'll have to do the right thing, too. She'll believe you, even if she didn't believe me."

"She will?"

"Keeping quiet was wrong. But I knew I couldn't accuse them alone. Now it won't be just my word against theirs. It'll be yours, too. We have proof, right here." She points at the phone, then nods in the direction of my bike. "Do you want a ride home? We can figure out what to do next. Who to talk to."

I shake my head and stand, sliding the phone into my back pocket. She could ask for it and I would give it to her. The proof.

Why doesn't she ask for it? Take it. Make the choice for me.

"It won't fit . . . probably . . . in your trunk."

Each slow step I take away from Bean feels impossibly heavy. When I finally reach my bike and get on, it creaks. Like it always does.

"Okay," she says. "Probably not. But I'll call you tomorrow. We'll talk. Until then . . . get home safe."

"I will," I say, already pushing off on my pedal. "Night, Bean."

When I pass Jen's house again, I don't get off my bike. I don't look at the house.

I just ride away as fast as I can, knowing why Bean didn't ask me for the phone.

She thinks I'll do the right thing.

SPRING

THE HOUSE OVERFLOWED. PEOPLE sat on the counters in the kitchen. Danced in the family room and spilled out onto the deck. Lined up for beer on the grass and milled anywhere they could find space.

My phone buzzed nonstop as people posted and tagged photos of me and Jen and Selena and Bean, me and them, online. I held a red cup half full of water because as long as it looked like I was drinking no one gave me a hard time about it. Like Steven, who had just asked if the beer had finally loosened me up. I'd responded with a silent glare.

Even though I wasn't drinking, my limbs naturally began to feel like a paper Halloween skeleton, joints held together with brass fasteners, flinging this way and that. My laughter came quicker as the night wore on. It was hard not to get caught up in everyone's good mood: summer freedom was here. For some, it was the end of their years in this town, the first of the last parties before college. For others, it was a respite before the hard farm labor that would fill their summers.

Bean had stripped to her swimsuit and was laughing at someone's joke in the hot tub.

"Come in with us," Jen called across the lawn to me from just inside the back door as she headed in to change into her own bikini.

I shrugged and turned back to Bean. Someone splashed her playfully and she slapped a wave of water back then held up her hands to shield herself. She giggled herself into hiccups. The bottom of her hair was curling from dampness.

"Later," I told Jen.

She was at my elbow. Someone bumped my back as they stumbled across the deck, pushing me into Jen. It was hard to hear Jen with all the shouting and laughing around us. "No," she said. "Now. Come on. There won't be a lot of laters with you in a year, remember?"

"Like you said at the river party, we have a whole *year.*"

"A whole *nothing* if you would just stop being such a baby and come to college with me."

"*I'm* the baby? You're the one who's scared to go alone."

We watched Bean climb out of the hot tub and slip into her dress and flip-flops.

Jen elbowed me in the ribs. "Don't be a jerk. You could at least apply to a few schools. Just in case you come to your senses."

"And waste my time and application fees? I *know* I'm staying here. What's the point?"

"The point is what if you change your mind?" Jen's voice was rising. Her cheeks splotched pink. This wasn't her talking; it was everything she'd had to drink. Or else this *was* her, and the alcohol was finally letting her say it. "The point is you're being stupid and throwing your whole life away on this town when there's a whole world out there."

"I'm not going to change my mind." My voice rose, too. I paused. Took in the flush on her neck. Then softer, "I'm sorry, Jen."

"Sure you are." She yelled the last of it. "You don't *get* it. No one requires anything from you! You can stay . . . go . . . who cares? But with me . . . everything I do is measured. Against—" Jen pressed her lips together. Both our glances shifted to where her brother stood.

I didn't say anything for a second. "Then it'll be *good* for you to get out," I whispered.

Her eyes met mine. Glassy with the things she didn't admit to anyone very often. "Whatever, Kayla." She turned back to the house, gathering her hair in a ponytail as she walked.

I turned away and looked for Bean again.

She was far enough across the lawn that I couldn't see her any longer. Or else she'd turned the corner at the stables. It was where I wanted to be, I realized. With my gentle horse. Away from all the noise here. The night had grown, suddenly, too stressful. Too full of movement. Too claustrophobic.

The sounds of the party faded steadily as I picked my way across the grass. One heel in front of the other, balancing on the front of my shoes so the backs didn't sink into the soil. The sequins that had been so pretty on the hanger scratched painfully at the delicate, inside skin of my upper arms. A spring wind plucked hair in groups of three and four strands from my updo and whipped them across my face; a few stuck in the gloss over my lips.

A horse snorted. It didn't sound like Caramel Star, but I wasn't sure which one it was. I could barely hear anyone from the party anymore, as though my ears had been submerged in water. My chest was hot from my argument with Jen; I sucked in breath after cool breath, willing my muscles to relax. The tall, dark outline of the barn loomed above me. I heard someone laughing.

"Bean?" I called.

Sitting with Bean, letting her calmness wash over me. That was what I needed.

But there was something else in the air. It was nothing I could point to: the smell of the horses was right, the stars overhead were right, the rising chorus of night insects the farther I moved from the party. Everything was *right*.

But when I walked into the barn, I heard other sounds. Muffled laughter again.

Muffled . . . something else. Not laughter. Something desperate.

I reached the corner of the barn where I knew, if I turned, I'd find the source. Dragged my fingertips across the weathered wood, catching my pinkie on a tiny splinter. There was a glow around the bend. Just the hint of light. Voices. Boys.

I rounded the corner, Bean's name soft on my lips.

FALL

IT FEELS LIKE PINS pricking my skin, waiting for Bean to call. I wander the house like a ghost, pouring then slowly slurping at a bowl of cereal. Washing my hands in the bathroom too long, the warm water running over and over my fingers. Drying them and the skin feeling uncomfortably tight. Hanging in my closet the dress I'd tossed on the floor last night, then changing my mind and stuffing it in the garbage.

My head pounds.

When will she call? I ask the Kayla in the mirror as I swallow aspirin and a glass of orange juice.

Turn off your phone, I tell the Kayla who sits on the edge of her bed in a daze, instead of finishing the homework due on Monday.

I don't turn off my phone. I stop waiting and call Bean. Her phone rings, but she never answers. Where is she?

What is she doing?

Leave the house, says the Kayla who doesn't answer when her brother, sitting beside her on the couch and staring at the TV, asks a question. *Run.*

Caleb nudges me in the arm. Ella opens one lazy dog eye to watch us.

"What?"

"Dude, wake up. You're like a zombie. I was asking what time we should go over. I don't want crappy seats."

"Soon," I say. I reach over and let one of Ella's smooth ears slip through my fingers. My body feels like an anthill, millions of little bugs scurrying inside. "Now."

He raises an eyebrow. It's still two hours until the homecoming game starts. Steven's phone is upstairs and I swear I can hear the video playing through the floorboard above my head. The telltale . . . something.

I stand and reach for my shoes in the entryway. Force my voice not to shake. "We'll join some tailgaters. Get your jacket. Let's go."

The parking lot for the community center across the street from the high school is half full when we arrive. Smoke rises from the grills. The sound of sizzling sausages and smell of barbecue sauce fill the air. Caleb's feet have barely hit the ground before he's grabbed by former classmates with cans of cheap beer. I follow him to a corner of trucks, where a portable radio is broadcasting the local college game and a table is set with chips and Jell-O shots in our school colors of red and gold. I toss one back when no one is looking.

In the next hour, the lot fills to capacity and soon after overflows down the road. Selena joins me first, then Jen. But I can't stop looking around for Bean because she has to be somewhere, doing something, and I need to know what. How much time before Jen and Selena find out what I know?

How long before the false safety I've built around myself crumbles? People start putting away their grills and Bean's entire family still isn't here. It could be that they just decided not to come to the game this year. Or there's something else keeping them home. A sick cow. Family movie night.

"I know you never drink, but you should try one of these before they all get packed up," Selena says, holding yet another Jell-O shot toward me. "They're good. Plus school spirit and all that."

I nod dazedly at Serena's mischievous smile, squeeze the little plastic cup into my mouth and swallow. She laughs, surprised. "That's a first."

My feet are starting to feel light.

I've stopped caring about Bean.

The first row of seats is reserved for Jay's family. As Selena and I sit behind them, I crane my neck around to look for my parents and almost lose my balance. I see Caleb about a dozen rows back with some of his friends, but my mom and dad aren't here. I check my phone for a text, but there's nothing telling me the rest of my family is running late.

I look up because the crowd begins to get antsy, like a tiny electric current is traveling the length of the bleachers. With a blast that vibrates in my ears, the marching band announces its presence. As the uniformed musicians take the field, we rise to our feet and roar. I clutch Selena's sleeve to remain steady.

The biggest game of the year is about to begin.

* * *

Just before halftime, we are ahead by one touchdown with Highland Hills High at our fifteen yard line. Their quarterback has been giving Jay a run for his money, but confidence in our star player hasn't waned. On the next play, Highland Hills throws an interception and our fans go wild. Grant High's defensive team jogs off the field, to be replaced by our offense. They form a circle, waiting for Jay to join them and give directions. We have less than a minute to create a bigger lead going into the second half of the game. Momentum is key.

Jay's taking a really long time to get on the field.

"Geez, Jay, can't it wait?" Selena mutters.

I follow her gaze, tilting my head to see around the slew of coaches and players on the sideline. I'd watched the first quarter of the game as a blur, but as the shots wore off, the players became clearer.

Jay's on his cell phone. He turns his back to the field, realizes there are hundreds of people in that direction, too, and positions himself parallel to the field, holding his hand over his mouth and phone so whoever he's talking to can hear him. The sun glints off the Roman warrior emblazoned on the helmet sitting on the bench beside him.

Suddenly, he shoves his phone into his bag and grabs the strap with a strong fist, knocking over his helmet as he stumbles on a patch of grass, and by the time he's stood up

again, there are two police officers at the sidelines. I pull my
arms close to my body as all my muscles tense.

Jen, turning around to say something to us, notices what
we're looking at. Her mouth hangs open silently for a second
before she says, "Probably here for the halftime show."

I nod but I know better.

They're here, and Bean isn't.

I check my phone again. Nothing.

The officers spot Jay and walk over to him before he can
get onto the field.

It's taken a very long time from interception to this point.
Days, it feels like. My blood is thickening like fudge. I hold
my breath. The field spins as though I had twice as many
Jell-O shots. Beside me, Selena sniffs. A shiver runs up my
spine.

And then one cop moves behind Jay and tilts her head
down close to his. Says something. Puts two fingers on his
elbow, just barely, and tries to move him along. As though
she doesn't want to cause a scene. As though thousands of
people aren't watching. But the coaches run toward them,
mouths open, screaming. One coach throws his clipboard on
the ground and flings a finger in the cop's face. Players on the
field come rushing back to the sidelines. Two more officers
approach and I can't see Jay for the shoulders and shouts and
rushing family members obscuring him from view.

I am suddenly alone in my section. The field is a riot.

Another cop pulls out handcuffs and tries to hurry Jay out of there. I get a two-second peek of Jay, his arms behind his back, his face expressionless.

There is panic among the coaches. People trying to shut them up, hold them back. A wall of football fans forms across the exit, arguing with the officers trying to get through with Grant High's star player. The officers patiently wave their arms, there is shoving, there is shouting, there is a call for backup.

But it's not for the player in handcuffs. Jay is calm. All he does is scan the crowd. When his eyes fall on me, he pauses. Even from here the blue of his eyes is piercing. Clear and calculated.

The shiver in my back expands until my shoulders are trembling and goose bumps rise along my arms. We could be the only two people here, the way all noise and movement around me cease. I want to call across the stands, ask him if he remembers saying he would dedicate this football season to me.

Jay works the muscle in his jaw once, tears his eyes away from me, and lets the officers move him out of the stadium. Before he is completely out of sight, I see him flash his coaches, the cheerleaders, the fans, his *aw-shucks* grin.

I don't move as the crowds slowly find their seats again and the second string quarterback is brought onto the field. There is still a game to play, even though the stands are thick with confusion. Jen's family doesn't return and neither does Selena. It's cold in my empty row.

The halftime show is weirdly subdued and the marching band can't seem to agree on one tempo. The dance team looks like they forgot to choreograph their performance. I've lost sight of where I am. There is too much color and not enough oxygen and the white lines on the field bleed into the green of the grass and the red of the uniforms; everything looks like mud and blood.

Caleb appears beside me, says something. The stands are emptying. At some point, the game ended.

Caleb packs in the next room. He's too quiet. I need slamming doors right now. Something to distract my brain. It's too busy racing, reliving Jay in handcuffs, the ride home in a quiet sort of panic. There's a mania to the way my eyelids flutter, my feet pace the room, my fingers clench and unclench fists.

Not knowing what else to do, I brush my hair and I want to pull it tight, tightly, tighter. Anything to keep from wondering where Bean is right now, from trying to imagine the way Jen feels right now. Anything painful to take the place of the staggering in my chest, the heady pressure that hasn't faded since the arrest stole the air from the stands.

But nothing hurts enough for that.

"I'm leaving." Caleb pokes his head in my room. He

balances on one foot for a second, lopsided as he tries to even out his thoughts.

There's so much he could say, could ask. *Who are you, Kayla? I should have warned you, Kayla. Kayla . . . about Hailey . . . about that night last spring.*

But he goes with: "I guess I'll see you soon?"

"Maybe."

I told him yesterday that I *might* drive to Missouri State to visit over Veterans Day weekend. It would depend on whether I can get behind the wheel of a car without hyper-ventilating.

Caleb crosses my floor and squeezes me in a big-brother hug.

"You should try. It'd be good for you. To get behind the wheel again. Try to be . . . normal." He pulls away, giving me an encouraging smile. "Let me know either way."

I nod. If I could wrap my head around my thoughts I might say more to him about how great it's been to see him, how much I enjoyed the view from Point Fellows on our hike, how I get it. *I get it now.* But I don't.

"Drive safe," I say.

"I'll call when I get there."

I stand at my window and watch Caleb's truck lights cut through the twilight and then they're down the road and out of sight and all I can see are the lights left on at the houses across the fields.

My mom materializes in the doorway. She keeps her hands occupied by wiping them nervously on a dish towel, again and again. "Do you want to talk?"

Dad is reorganizing his spotless shed out back. Again.

A truck comes up the road. Because he is where I am when I need him. As though he knows everything. But he can't know everything, because if he did, he would never come again.

He is too good for that. For secrets. For me.

"I have to go," I say.

Mom bites the inside of her bottom lip for a second and I feel sure she's going to say no, to make me stay home so that I'll talk to her.

"Don't be out late," she says as Noah pulls into the drive and waits.

I nod and go down to meet him.

I climb in his truck and don't speak until after we've pulled out of the driveway. My arms are wrapped around my ribs and my tongue pauses on the tip of a sharp canine.

Noah seems relaxed, breathing slowly while I force my arms not to shake.

He stares straight ahead. The tips of his shaggy hair curl just slightly at the back of his ears, disappearing into the dark crease behind the lobe.

"Kayla—" he begins.

"Shh," I cut him off.

He twists his head to catch my eye and my lungs ache at the breath held captive there; it threatens to whoosh out at the hurt in his expression but I release it slowly.

His name is on the tip of my tongue, the letters writing themselves across my lips should I only open them. I long to tell him that he made me feel like it was possible to come home again, easy to be the Kayla I liked. And that if he knew the truth, all that would change.

My lashes flutter in a series of quick blinks. My head begins to spin like a carnival ride.

"I can't talk about . . . that," I say.

And when he looks at me again, there's a new understanding in his expression. Maybe even sympathy. Because my involvement, he knows, must be complicated.

My involvement *is* complicated.

"What do you want to do, then?" he says.

"Can we go to the river? Just walk for a while."

"Sure."

There is a milky quality to the sky. Like drifts of cotton floating to the stars. The air is sharp, brittle, and cold when I breathe through my nose. The quiet is small-town quiet: the white-noise musical insects and the whoosh-rush of a river.

He takes my hand and we walk a little until we find a patch of soft grass, then sit. The blades tickle the sides of my neck when I lie back and I remember a moment like this from a lifetime ago with three girls and thinking life was perfection, that it could never change.

"I belonged here once," I say.

Noah stretches his body out beside me. We are almost the same height. I like that our shoes are placed to nudge against each other. That our knees line up. That when I turn my head, my eyes go right to his mouth. "Why do we try so hard to belong?"

"You do realize you're asking *me* that question, right?" Noah laughs softly.

"Did you ever want to belong . . . more?"

"Who doesn't want to belong to their home? I used to beat myself up about it. Almost as much as those other guys beat me up." He laughs again.

I close my eyes, wanting to forget that ever happened to him.

"I hated that my mom came from someplace different, the way she looked, the way *I* looked, that she grew things in our garden that nobody else did. I hated that she took me away from here for a while. It was important to her that I know my roots, but I didn't care. But then I stopped hating myself, you know? For all these different reasons. It takes a lot of energy to hate where you come from. Too much." Noah gathers a handful of grass and begins stripping the blades in two.

"It takes a lot of energy to love it, too," I say. "Sometimes

I feel exhausted. Like this town sucks everything out of me. And for some reason . . . I'm willing to give it everything."

"Does it? I didn't know that. I feel very . . . neutral about this town." He lets the grass fall back to the earth through his fingers. "I don't want to give everything to this place. I'm never going to be like the other people here, but I've decided that's okay. I don't have to look a certain way or play certain sports or eat certain things to be okay. I can do my own thing." He shrugs. "I'll get out of here soon enough, so in some ways it's just about biding my time."

"But isn't that lonely?"

"I have friends, Kayla. People call me quiet. They think I'm invisible. But they don't realize that I've just chosen who and what's important to me. . . ." His voice hitches and I wonder if he means me, at all. I want him to mean me. "I ignore all the rest. And they don't even see how doing that is subversive."

"I see you," I say, turning my head to look at him. "I'm sorry I didn't before. I'm sorry I ever stopped seeing you. I was wrong."

"The only thing that's making me start to regret not caring about this town . . . is you."

He raises his hand and tangles his fingers in my hair. My hands go to his strong shoulders as he angles himself halfway over me. And when he kisses me, it doesn't matter if either of us belongs or if we're invisible to everyone outside this riverbank. All that matters is the realness of us, here, right now.

We stay on the banks of the river until the night chorus awakens and river-chill sets in. When he drives me home, our small talk interspersed with lingering breaks is as comfortable as it can be with all the thoughts lurking at the edges of my mind. Our hands, clasped in the center of the seat, are warm. When we turn onto Sunview, a heaviness comes over me.

It never used to feel this way. Coming home from anywhere—a doctor's appointment, a competition, spring break in Florida—once rejuvenated me. Now, I want to slump in my seat and hide.

"Hey," Noah says when we get to my house. "I know you don't want to talk yet about what's going on. But are you going to be okay?"

I tug on the bottom of my hair. It feels like past time for honesty. "I don't know."

"It's going to be okay." His hand reaches for the back of my neck and he draws me to him and I press my forehead to his and wonder why he gets to get away with lying. It's not okay—I can't ever see a time when it will be okay. But he kisses me and for a few seconds, it's better.

SPRING

"OH MY GOD."

I froze.

The boys froze, too. Steven, with his fucking camera. Jay and that beer bottle.

The part of the beer bottle I could see. Over the top of Bean's slender, white thigh, disappearing into blackness. Her hand moved dazedly up and down, swatting at Jay, but she couldn't reach him where he sat back on his heels, the grin slowly fading from his face.

"Shit." The phone light went out and our eyes adjusted to the dark in silence.

"Kayla?" Bean turned her face to me, rolled her eyes in my direction. Mascara smeared across her cheeks. Hair clung to her temples. She put a hand down on the ground beside her, quickly, trying to keep her balance. A sob escaped her. She heaved once. Twice. Tried to kick at Jay, who was on his feet by now. Another sob and my name again, drawn out in two awful, heartbroken syllables.

The ice that had taken over my veins melted. Slowly at first, then rapidly, stoked by anger, fury, rage.

"Get your car," Jay's voice said.

Steven took off for the house.

I stepped forward, fists clenched and raised. My mind was in a free fall, and I couldn't capture any real thought but the need to hit Jay and to claw his face and press my nails into his eyes and come away with blood.

He met me halfway. His hands curled around my arms, digging into the flesh underneath my biceps and I was certain he was going to rip the muscle and tendon from the bones and I cried out from the pain and the need to destroy him.

Bean got to her hands and knees, and where her dress was still hunched up around her hips, I could see a dark streak. If Jay hadn't been holding me up by my arms I would have fallen to my knees and gathered Bean to me.

"Shut the fuck up, Kayla," Jay said, because I'd screamed, as if anyone could have heard it over the sounds of the party. But I took another breath to scream again. It faltered into a moan as his fingers tightened on me. "You don't even know what's going on here."

Jay pulled me hard, away from Bean, out of the barn, toward Nickerson Road on the far east border of the Brewster property. I managed to turn my head and I saw the party fading into the landscape. His strides were long and sure, and I tripped behind him because he would drag me, I knew, if I fell.

I saw a car driving on the road alongside the Brewster property and then bumping over the shallow trench divider between the gravel and the grass, coming onto the fields before stopping abruptly in front of us.

Steven got out, leaving the engine running, and Jay pulled me around to the driver's seat. His hand was atop my head, so fucking heavy, like a concrete block, pushing my neck, every vertebra in my spine down, down, down, compressing my whole body into something inches tall, too small for my lungs to find room to expand. I gasped at air, smelled the beer on Jay's breath. I couldn't get enough oxygen. Any.

Jay shoved me forward, and I wasn't quite small enough because the side of my head collided with the frame of the door and bursts brighter than the stars exploded across the darkness of my vision. He slammed the door closed. I reached for the handle and pushed, but Steven blocked it from the outside.

"Drive," Jay said as he slid into the passenger side and held my right arm, keeping me in place. Steven jumped in the back.

"Or what?!" I screamed.

"Just drive down Nickerson." His voice was calm, except for the telltale way his "v" sound was slightly slurred. Even after everything else, he wouldn't drive drunk. My brain twisted maniacally, focusing on stupid thoughts like that, instead of formulating a plan, figuring out what to do to get out of here and help Bean. I needed to . . . I needed to . . . His fingers dug into my bicep again.

I crumpled into the driver's seat. Steven's battered old

Ford. My palm hovered over the stick shift and I concentrated on commanding my hand to stop shaking and grip it. I blinked red haze.

Jay reached his other arm forward and I thought he was going to grab me so I yelped, but he was just turning the music off. I wanted to put my seat belt on. An oddly clear idea when every other thought made me feel like shattering. But I was afraid of making any movement that Jay hadn't told me to. I ground the gear into first and pressed on the gas so hard the car lurched forward. I squinted into the distance, trying to find the road until the car bounced over the unevenness of gravel.

"You'll keep your mouth shut. You didn't see anything," Jay said. His voice was slurred but hard.

"Uh, yeah, she did." Steven. From the backseat.

Jay turned around and smacked him. "She didn't see anything!" he yelled.

"I didn't see anything," I repeated. I didn't know what I was saying. All I knew was that I needed time.

I had seen everything. *Everything.* People would know about it. I'd make sure of that.

But we were driving. Where? Why? Where did they want me to drive them?

Jay took his hands off me. Rolled the beer bottle between his palms and looked at me. "You're a good girl. My sister's best friend." He stopped.

A good girl. His sister's best friend. In the part of my head that was swimming with hope, I understood that to mean he wouldn't . . . couldn't . . . do anything to me. But the rest of my mind was suffocated with images of what he did to another of his sister's best friends. To another good girl.

"She wanted that," he said. He slammed the bottle against the dashboard. Glass flew everywhere.

"Dude!" Steven yelled. "My car!"

"It's a piece of shit." Jay laughed.

Out of the corner of my eye, I saw the jagged, sharp-teeth edge of the bottle. If I told what I'd seen—and if that meant his life as he imagined it could be over—how hard would he try to keep me quiet? How much could my life have meant to him?

I shifted into fourth, carefully keeping the car steady on slick, oily gravel. We were leaving the field landscape and approaching a stand of trees, thin and spindly at first but thickening quickly.

Maybe miles behind us now, Bean was crying, alone, sprawled in the dirt. Or crawling back to the house. I prayed that whoever found her first would, please God, do something to help her.

I had to do something. I had to get out of this car. I had to stop them.

My eyes felt glued to the road, as though if I looked away for one second I could lose the tiny bit of control I had being in the driver's seat. As if they'd finally realize I could turn back, drive where *I* wanted to go, not them, do *something*. If only I could push through that panic and figure out what. But a movement in my peripheral vision commanded my attention. I turned my head. Jay brushed the tip of a bottle shard across his thumb. Shadows glinted off the glass and then in his eye when he slowly looked over at me.

A sound halfway between a sob and a cough escaped my mouth.

I had to save myself. Then save Bean. Like the way the flight attendants said on planes: put my oxygen mask on first then help others. In the strange mix of wild and calm in my head, crashing the car was the right thing to do. If I turned into the ditch so that the tree hit their side . . . blocked their doors. I would have time. Enough to get back.

Our eyes locked.

He saw everything in the set of my mouth, in the dark hate in my eyes, in the white of my knuckles around the steering wheel.

"Bitch—" He lunged across the car for me. His whole body: foot wedged in and slammed into mine on the gas pedal, hands over hands. But I had already turned the car and the gravel was so accommodating, loving these kids and the doughnuts they pulled on this road late at night and it was as easy as falling into a cloud.

Steven's car always spun beautifully.

The truck cresting the hill just ahead of us tried to spin, too. The truck almost managed to turn enough, its headlights cutting across the surprise on my face for less than a second. It turned far enough away to hit the back of our car instead of the front, connecting with metal and glass and Steven's flesh and bones. The doors on my side flung open and gravel and bark embedded in my skin everywhere and the hood slammed into a tree and blood slammed into my head and my chin slammed into the ground. Salty warmth burst over my teeth.

There was no lingering car horn, only a vague memory that the truck had blared its horn before we crashed. There were no voices, only the vague idea that some voices might be silenced for good.

I looked up to see a small dark object within arm's reach. My right arm wouldn't move, no matter how much I willed it to, but my left hand finally grabbed the phone. *Evidence.* I took it and fumbled it into my shorts pocket.

And I promised everything to Bean before letting the song of the cicadas lull me to sleep.

FALL

MOM'S HALFWAY UP THE stairs when I come in and she asks how my drive was.

"All right. We just went to the river for a walk."

She watches me closely until I turn away. How much does she read from my face, gone pale, from my hands clutching my upper arms? Probably everything.

My phone chimes at me as Mom's steps recede and I dig it out of my pocket.

It's still not Bean.

"There's still going to be a bonfire tonight," Jen says.

"I'm pretty tired," I tell her.

"We've barely . . . and you're already ditching me?"

I stick one hand in the back pocket of my jeans and look out the window next to the front door. I don't want to ditch Jen, but I also don't want to see her right now. It doesn't feel good. Thinking I'm going to do the right thing doesn't make the likelihood that I'll lose Jen again hurt any less.

She takes my hesitation as the okay and I let her because, God, it hurts to think of these as our last moments, but it's even worse to think our last moments have already passed.

"I'll pick you up in half an hour," she says.

* * *

I slip out the back door and Jen picks me up half a mile down the road from my house. I didn't tell my parents I was heading out. Something tells me they won't want to know. A ghost whisper in the air: *Keep your daughters close.*

Selena takes up the front passenger seat in Jen's compact SUV so I squeeze in the back, pushing aside a pile of school papers and horse brushes.

"Jay needs the big one for his football equipment," Erica Brewster had said on Jay and Jen's sixteenth birthday, even though Jen hadn't asked for an explanation as they both stood on their driveway and took in their presents, side by side. Never mind that Jen's riding equipment took up more room than Jay's football pads.

It should feel roomy, but the ceiling threatens to cave in on me. I am stifled by the things the three of us know and aren't talking about.

After a couple of minutes of driving, we catch up to another familiar SUV. My chest caves in on itself when I realize Jay's out already. Gliding through town in front of us. Did they even question him at all?

I lose count of the number of heads I see bouncing around inside through the rear window of his truck as we trail him. The windows are rolled down to take advantage of cool autumn air. The people we pass on our way don't care that the music is obnoxiously loud or that there are more people in his car than seat belts. They grin and wave.

They're just boys out having a good time.

The farther we get from Third Street, the more my stomach tightens. Jen is quiet, her fingers tapping anxiously on the steering wheel. Selena stares out the window.

I realize the music in Jay's car has been turned off and the heads aren't bobbing around anymore. The boys are still.

Clouds roll in and windows roll up and we keep driving. We pass two crumbling concrete silos on the left. My teeth grind together. We take a right. There are only two farms out on this road, and I can't come up with a reason for us all to visit old Mr. and Mrs. McNaughton.

"The bonfire's behind the community center," I say. I'm reminded of a night this past spring and a panic that made my thoughts trip over one another. "We're going to Bean's."

Jen gives me a sharp look in the rearview mirror. Selena doesn't move.

"Why are we going there?" I ask.

"Because Jay said let's go make nice, Kayla."

The cars pull off the road, parking parallel to the cross-fenced field behind Bean's house. I've seen her cows grazing out here before. When we were friends. They aren't here now. Tucked away for the night.

Boys start piling out of Jay's car.

Jen cuts her engine and hops out. "Let's go."

Selena and I are slower to move, hesitating with our fingers on the handles. After Jen shuts her door, I swallow.

There's going to be a bonfire tonight.

Selena folds her arms across her chest and looks to the distance. "Bean filed a report."

"Obviously." I stare at the sky so she can't see the way my hands are shaking. The clouds are thick now.

"Did you get your memory back or something?" she asks.

I toy with a loose piece of broken fingernail. She wants to know what I know. She wants to know if I know what she knows. If we're the same.

"I've known for a long time. Since Kansas City."

Selena's fingers move along the underside of the bottom hem of her dress, pulling at loose threads. When she realizes she's ruining her skirt, she rubs her palms on her knees and shakes her head.

Selena meets my eyes in the rearview mirror. In them, I see steeliness. Unshed tears. Shame, because we want to be safe more than we want justice for one of our best friends.

Apprehension, because Bean has broken the rule of silence.

And the understanding that we have to pick sides.

This is why Selena and Bean aren't best friends anymore. Because Selena's self-preservation is stronger than her loyalty to her best friend.

I think about the smells of wet grass and the freshness of moving water down by the river. I think about the taste and comfort of Mom's Sunday dinners and the Mayan Revenge at Toffey's. I think about the sounds of cheering at football games and the whinnies of the horses in Jen's barn.

I think about my time in Kansas City, feeling like my insides had been turned inside out with missing home. How the air there didn't fill my lungs like the air here does. How my aunt was nice, but that she wasn't my mom.

"I won't tell Jen about this. About . . . what you don't know."

I'm reminded of a night this past spring and an anger that set my chest ablaze. I say, "She was your best friend."

Finally, Selena moves. Just enough to stiffen her shoulders. "*Don't*. She was your best friend, too. But here we are." Her chin swivels toward me. "Because we both know, that what they're going to do to her? They'd do it to us, too."

I'm reminded of a night this past spring when Jay looked at the broken glass in his hand and then looked at me. When my thoughts blurred with fear about what he could do to me. When I made a choice that ended up killing a boy.

I can't grasp what logic it was that led me here now. Hiding a souvenir of that night. Silently defending those boys after what they did to her, to me. Fear has pushed logic aside.

"Us, our families . . . So, shut the fuck up and get out of the car, Kayla," Selena finishes.

I try twice to grab the door handle before it takes and I slide into the overgrown grasses at the side of the road. When my feet touch down, a whoop rends the sky.

"Go, go, go!" Senior Brian White, the kicker on the football team, screams as a horde of boys hurdle the fence and dash for the barn. One of them carries a plastic red jug.

Moonlight pokes through the clouds for one split second, landing on Jay like grace from heaven, like it's supposed to, and I bite back a scream. Jen and Selena sit atop the fence but I put my hands on it and my foot on it and I don't try to lift myself up.

Bean's brother, Eric, comes tearing out of his house as the boys start throwing gasoline on the barn. His mouth is open but I can't hear him over the others and I want to scream at him to go back, stay away, to save himself, but he won't hear me over the others, either.

How often did Caleb think he was protecting Eric when he kept his silence?

When the guys see him, two grab him and hold his arms behind his back. He struggles and squirms. He's fifteen, but tiny.

Jay isn't the one who does the honors. It's T. J. who lights and drops the matches. One, two, I lose count, as he walks around the barn lighting and dropping matches.

Dry wood catches quickly. I love the smell of burning wood, but tonight it is laced with gasoline and something worse, too. It burns my lungs.

I trip over the road before I realize I've been slowly walking backward while watching the burning barn.

"He's saying . . ." Jen swallows, and I know it tastes like smoke and I wonder what else it tastes like. If it's bitter and acidic like the flavors in my mouth. "That the cows are still in there."

Where is Bean? Where are Bean's parents? I hope they are far, far away.

Selena stares at the ground, flicking her phone on and off repeatedly.

Jen watches, flames reflected in her glazed-over eyes.

Me . . . I am not like Jen. I can't look.

And yet, I am these people and this is my home and I am complicit.

I belong.

The barn crackles and pops, sending sparks high into the sky. Some of the guys have retreated closer to the fence, but the others stand close, still holding on to Bean's little brother, who is trying to hold back sobs in front of the older boys.

My nostrils are thick with smoke; Selena's eyes are hard and shimmering.

Jen's hair is pulled back in a tight, low bun. It makes her eyes look enormous. Or maybe, I think, that's just the intense way she's staring right at me.

The impulse I had to run to Kansas City after the accident is nothing like the compulsion to run away that I have at this moment.

I don't understand how this could have happened. How

one night could have ruined all of us. I want to be able to go back to my best friend as she was. To all my friends. To my perfect, perfect home. The place it was before that party.

The place, I know now, it never really was.

I've taken several steps backward.

"Where are you going?" Jen says.

I shake my head and wrap my arms around myself. "The smell is bothering my throat."

"You're going to ditch me. . . ."

The same argument. Just like that. Like nothing happened.

My fingers clench into fists. "How can you do this? How can you *know* and just . . . be here now? Watching them do this!"

Jen's hands go to her forehead and I think she's going to crumble, but then they smooth over the top of her head and she calmly begins to unwind her bun. "I'm not the one doing it," she says.

"Jen. Oh my God. Listen to you."

"*Me*, Kayla?"

"Yes, you! Pretending you're not part of this, just because you didn't light the match. Like nothing happened to one of our *best friends*."

Flames' shadows lick across Jen's face. "I have to be here . . . I have to do this." She clears her throat. "I'm caught between Bean and my family. I have nowhere to go. No auntie to cry to. What am I *supposed* to do? How am I supposed to react when a night gets out of hand? When everyone has something different to say about it?"

"It wasn't just *that night*, Jen. And Bean is one of us!" I scream.

Jen throws up her hands. "*Us?* What does that mean? Because in the morning, this town will be split into two sides. Bean on one and Jay on the other." A tiny gasp escapes and here it is. A release of all the things she's known these past months and never said. They make her scream: "And my side has been picked for me!"

"It doesn't have to be. . . ."

Except for her, it does. And that's when I look at Selena. At the way she covers her face with her hands, the way her shoulders shake.

Jen drags the back of her hand across her face. "But *you*. You get to choose. You can choose me and Selena and whatever it is you see in that guy Noah and your parents and your brother. Or you can choose to tell. And have *nothing*."

I take a breath. "I'll have—"

"*Nothing!* Because I can promise you that people will take Jay's side. To them, you'll be a liar and a slut and God knows what else. And those people who will want Jay's head on a stake? They'll want nothing to do with the girl who sat on that secret for months, either. And that's not even counting all the people who will realize the accident wasn't as much of an accident as you let them believe it was. There's only one way you can win."

I stare at her with my mouth hanging open, my insides as cold as my skin. *Killer Kayla.*

We're both quiet for a minute.

I pull out my cell phone and back away. I call the fire department. The woman on the line doesn't ask how the fire started or who set it, only where it is. If there is anyone in the barn.

"No people," I say.

"Are you a safe distance from the fire?" she asks.

"Yes."

"Assistance is on its way. Please stay where you are until help arrives."

I ignore her. I hang up then call home, walking down the road, away from the fire engulfing Bean's barn. And into the flames filling me.

The sky opens on the drive home and I hope it helps put out the fire fast enough to save the cows. Raindrops batter the windshield of my mom's car, but I don't mind because the noise covers the sound of my legs shaking against my seat. I will the car to go faster, take the curves in the road like a race car, run through the few stop signs. I want to be home.

I promised my mom when she picked me up I would tell her exactly what happened once the fire department was done putting out the fire. As the rain continues to fall, I hear Jen's words again and again. *The accident wasn't as much of an accident as you let them believe it was.*

I wonder if I will keep that promise to my mom. I've lost track of the promises I've made.

I lie back on my rug, staring at the way beams of light filter through my curtains. I've been here for hours. Long enough to see night turn to dawn turn to day. Closing my eyes plays scenes I don't want to see so I don't close them except to blink.

When slow steps begin on the stairs, I roll over, my back to the door. I've told my parents I'll be down soon. I just want to be alone now.

My door opens and I wait for one of their voices. Dad's low, soft timbre or Mom's confident declarations that at least I walked away from what they were doing at Bean's. At least I called her. It was a start.

It's neither of them.

"Your parents told me to come up. Are you awake?"

Noah must know I am from the way I suck in a breath and hold it, waiting. I keep my back to him because if I turn over and see his face and feel the warmth he radiates and talk to him, like we do, like I can, I don't know how I'll be able to go back to pretending.

But he crosses my room and sits on my bed, and in my

peripheral vision I see him taking up my old koala stuffed animal, tufting the fur on its ears, rubbing his thumb over its stomach.

"I know what it's like to carry a secret," he says. "At least . . ." He sets the koala down carefully, moving it a half inch to one side, then the other, obsessively looking for the center of my bed. "What I thought it might have been. I was never sure. I tried to get her to go to someone. The police. But Bean never said anything so I wasn't positive I was right about what happened. If I'd known for sure . . ."

"Because you were the one who drove her home that night," I say softly. Something I figured out a while ago but couldn't admit to myself. "Is that why you talked to me that first day of school? Because . . . you suspected and you thought I knew and . . ."

And *what*? Am I supposed to be upset?

Noah was the friend Bean needed all along, when the rest of us failed her.

I know I'm right because he doesn't answer.

Jen's right, too, and I've known it all along. If Noah knows what I am, the secrets I've kept, he will walk away. Because if he'd known for sure, he *would* have told.

He would be disgusted to know that losing him as a friend was on my list of reasons not to tell. That he could be a reason for me not to do the right thing.

He scratches the top of his ear and strands of hair fall

in his eyes. His shirt is open at his collarbone and I want to reach for the skin exposed there. With my fingers, with my lips.

When he raises his gaze to me, I look away. Certain the dark truth can be read in my eyes.

I pull my knees into my chest. "I can't."

And he doesn't even know what I'm talking about.

He nods. "Okay."

He moves off the bed, sits close to me. He strokes my head, once, and kisses my forehead, once.

His touch and his patience nearly undo me.

God, why can't he yell and rage at me and force me to action instead? But no . . . no, he can't make this decision for me or force me to be the good person I'm supposed to be.

I clutch at my shins, hold myself tightly even after the soft click of the door closing tells me he's left.

SPRING

ON THAT NIGHT IN May, I drove the car into the ditch on purpose.

Because I wanted to get away. Save myself. Then to get back to help Bean.

Maybe it would have been easier if all of us had died.

But no. Only one of us did.

Not me.

FALL

I PAINT, STROKE AFTER stroke, not stopping, even though paint fumes start to burn my eyes. It's an excuse for the tears.

My wrist hurts and my forearm feels dull so I switch hands and go at it lefty, splotching and splattering, letting the paint run in rivulets down the side of the boat I'd painstakingly sanded smooth.

I drop the brush in the grass and roll onto my back beside it, staring into the sun. When I can see nothing but black blobs surrounded by an aura of yellow-orange, I close my eyes and count the number of seconds until graduation. Days divided by hours divided by minutes divided by seconds . . . and it still feels too short, it still feels too long, the seconds nearly in the millions, too vast to comprehend.

My ankle throbs and so I try not to move, instead keeping still.

I run through all of it again, because I always do.

The fight Jen and I had, the long walk across the yard before I found Bean and Jay and Steven, blackness, blurriness. I'm behind the wheel of a car, Jay beside me, Steven behind me. Going somewhere, going nowhere. Sure, in that moment, they could have done anything to me.

Sure, in that moment, someone was going to get hurt.

Maybe die. Maybe me.

Jay sees it.

What I was about to do. The person I thought I was strong enough to be.

Don't they say that, in moments of desperation, we become stronger than we've ever been before? Strong enough to lift cars off bodies, to carry people to safety? To make a promise to save someone? To tell the truth when it's all over?

Eventually, though, that power fades, and we become mortal again.

The boat I spent all these months getting ready for the water is beautiful, a deep red. When I was in Kansas City over the summer, I looked forward to finishing the project. To having another thing to tie me to this town. This thing Jen and I found. This thing my dad and I built together. And now . . . being tied to this place is too dangerous.

I go to my room and grab a paper bag. Go to the garage for supplies. The boat is heavy, but I manage to drag it all the way onto the back of Dad's tractor, and I manage to drag it from the tractor to the river. The music of the water is lush, thick with humidity and the splash of leaping fish. It hasn't gotten cold yet. The boat slides in smoothly. I brace myself against the skiff with my palms while the fishermen watch me, puzzled.

I climb into the boat and set us off downstream, letting my hand drag off the side, in the water, wishing I could really forget. Wishing I never knew. Wishing there was nothing to know.

I press my nose into my shoulder, my breath gathering around my face gently. The hairs on the back of my neck stand upright.

When I can no longer see a fishing line, I dump out the contents of the bag from my closet into the boat and overturn the can of gasoline I'd brought. Slick, oily purple sequins.

Then I light a match and dive out of the boat before the flames can engulf me, and I swim for the shore.

When I get back home, Mom tells me the sheriff came by while I was gone, wanting to ask questions about that night last May. Someone . . . someone said I would know something.

"You smell like gas," she says, and there's a strange quality to her voice and I wonder if she's imagining Bean's barn burning down. My mom, who, if she knew the truth, would cast me back to Kansas City, if not farther away than that. There are limits, I think, to even how much a mother can love her daughter.

"Fumes from the boat." It's a lie and the truth at the same time.

"Do you want me to talk to the sheriff? Tell him you need some time? I know this is hard for you. She's one of your friends. I could take you over to see her—"

"No," I blurt out, without knowing why I'm refusing.

"Bean really needs a friend right now. To know people still love her. And I want you to hear something." Her eyes, soft brown, pierce into me and I wonder if mothers are all-knowing. "There are people here who love you, too. And who will keep loving you. No matter what."

I guess I wasn't who people thought I was, I want to say.

But the truth is, I do want to be that person. The good one. The friend.

I take a shower to get that gasoline smell off.

And when the fog clears from the mirror I can't look at myself.

SPRING

ON THAT NIGHT IN May, I drove the car into the ditch on purpose.

Because I wanted to save someone.

Not myself.

Not *only* myself.

FALL

I SIP AT ORANGE soda and watch the road until I see Noah's truck kicking up mud in the fading light of dusk.

He climbs the porch steps slowly, having seen my bike lying in the grass next to the driveway. His face as he peers around the column is guarded. "Are you okay?" he says.

"Things are going to change," I say.

"They will."

I wonder why I tried so hard the past few months to maintain something that was always going to slip through my fingers.

"It's a nice evening."

"Yeah," he says. Small-town weather talk.

"Will you take a hike with me?"

"A hike? Right now?"

"To Point Fellows."

"I've never been up there." He glances up, as though his reply is written in the cloudless sky. Then, "Okay."

I give Noah directions to Point Fellows over the music playing from his iPod and the wind rushing past the windows.

At the trailhead, I pause for a few moments, pretending to tie my shoelaces, looking around. This is the last time I'll be here, I know, for a long time. I memorize the colors of the leaves, the jutting of the rocks, the smell of the soil steeped in autumn's dampness.

I walk just ahead of Noah, squinting into the dying rays of the sun. My fingers curl, desperate to scratch the sweat that threatens to roll down the middle of my back. Or maybe there is no sweat. Maybe I just want to scratch this skin away in the hopes a different Kayla is underneath.

The landscape has changed since the last time I was here with Caleb. It's both drier and lusher at the same time. The trails are damper, but the river is skinnier.

It's something I love about home. That it is so many things at once. Others might see it as a fly-over state, but I know its charms.

I know what my home is.

What it was. Who my friends were. Who I loved and who loved me back.

At the top of the bluff, I sit and let my legs hang over the edge. Noah stands back a little, and I wonder if he's afraid of heights. But thoughts of him—of almost anything—fade when I pull the phone from my pocket.

It's not like I don't know. All I did in Kansas City last summer was read about rape statistics and wait for Bean to say something. I *wanted* her to say something. When she didn't, I started letting myself believe, sometimes, that I was wrong. That she might've been there because she'd wanted to be there. She told Steven sure, he could film it.

But I know the statistics. I know what "unreported" means.

We are taught fear, we girls.

But right now, I choose to push that fear away from me. I choose to own my actions and I choose to give up the place I love so much, for the promise that I will be able to love and live without fear one day.

I tighten my fingers around the phone and stare at the landscape, my home, until it blurs into one shade of gray.

God.

Why.

Why can't this town be the place I always wanted it to be?

All I wanted was to come home, to be a part of this town again. But I'm going to do the right thing. I'm going to be the friend to Bean I should have been all along.

Noah squats and watches me. Probably wondering about the phone I'm holding that isn't mine. His hand reaches out hesitantly, his fingers curling around mine.

I lean to the side and, without letting thoughts or nerves get in the way, brush my lips across his. My body sings with want and hunger for his mouth and his hands and his husky voice and the music he pulls from a few strings, but I pull away and my insides feel stone-thick and heavy.

"That's why you talked to me the first day of school," I say. My fingers play with his. Pressing their pads on his knuckles.

Rubbing across his palm. "To figure out what I knew."

He takes a slow breath. "Yes," he says. "Bean was always so nice to me. I wanted to make things better for her."

"The nicest girl ever," I say weakly.

"Kayla." He takes charge of our hands and threads his fingers through mine. "It's different now. I care about you. I learned that you don't remember, and I . . . really like being with you. I want to be with you."

"Noah." I swallow his name. Memorize his face, too. His kiss, his voice, his kindness, and patience. "No, you don't. I want to tell you something. Lots of things. But first, I want you to know that I didn't mean to kill Steven McInnis."

And I didn't. I wanted to stop him. Stop both of them. But not like that.

"I know you didn't," Noah says.

I press the back of his hand to my lips. "There's more."

And I tell him everything.

His fingers leave mine before I'm even done. He stands up when I'm almost finished. When I get to the part where Jay has his fingers around my arm and I think he'll separate the muscle from the bone, Noah's features pull with conflict, and the tiniest light of hope opens in my heart. But just as quickly he looks back down at the ground with what looks like disgust.

I pause because I'm crying too hard to continue and he must think I've said everything I'm going to say, because he walks far enough ahead of me back down the trail that he can't hear me talk or walk.

We climb into his truck and pull away. I squish myself against the passenger side door and roll down the window so that he doesn't have to breathe the same air as me.

I never get to tell him how I was trying to do the right thing that night. How I know, how I always knew, that I ended up doing all the wrong things anyway.

I can't tell him how much it meant that he spoke to me that first day of school. How much I liked having him in my life. How much I miss him already.

When I get back to my house, I slip the phone in an envelope, look up the new prosecutor's name and office phone number on my laptop, call, and leave a message. He must forward his calls to his personal line because he gets back to me in fifteen minutes. We arrange to meet the next morning at eight o'clock. He tells me I'm brave for coming forward. As if he understands more about our small town than we usually give outsiders credit for.

I feel, more than ever before, like a coward.

Bean came forward, against the advice of her family, of her best friend.

The way I should have months ago.

* * *

I stop in at Toffey's Coffees before I leave. It's empty on a Monday midmorning. People are at work. People are at school. Bean finally texted me to tell me she's leaving for California tomorrow.

There is safety in distance.

Noah Michaelson isn't behind the counter anymore. He told the prosecutor that he was the one who drove Bean home last May. That he saw how upset Bean was. How messed up. She hadn't told him, that night, what had happened, but he wondered and he worried. He knew for sure when Bean finally spoke up. When he talked to me.

Toffey's says he was let go for getting a customer's order wrong.

The new guy is toying with the strings of the small apron around his waist.

"Do you know how to make a Mayan Revenge?" I ask.

He pulls a face. "A what?"

I shake my head. "Never mind. I'll just have a vanilla latte."

He clicks the bean grinder and slams the espresso holder against the side of the counter. This may very well be the noisiest cup of coffee ever.

When he sets the finished product in front of me, there's a unicorn head outlined in my foam.

"Nice," I say dully, passing a bill to him.

He smiles, pleased, and punches a hole in a frequent buyer's card even though I haven't asked for one. "I've been practicing."

I tuck a dollar of my change into the tip jar and take my to-go cup, clutching hard to the painful burn against my palm.

My things are already packed in the car. I never did fully unpack from my last stay in Kansas City.

Dad drives and I think my last thoughts about home: the golden brown of spent cornfields, the earthy smell of hay, the slow turn of the river, Jen's dimple and sparkling eyes, the sun baking the gravel between Noah's house and mine, the gold of his skin and curve of his smile.

It's strange. When I left this town last May, it cut at me every day I was away. Now, though, I feel those wounds finally beginning to change. Still open but clean and maybe even on the path to healing.

When we get out of the car at my aunt's house, I hug my dad.

It's not stiff between us anymore, not since I came forward.

I hold my mom for a long time. I know that she loves me, that she'll be quick to forgive me, even if I don't know how long it will be before I can forgive myself.

And that's it. I won't graduate with the friends I'd called "best" my whole life. I won't have a bittersweet good-bye to say when we go our separate ways. I won't have Caramel Star to help keep me grounded and strong.

Everything feels light, like bubbling laughter.

You were right to tell. The text comes while I'm still standing in the doorway, watching my parents drive away. *To tell me. To tell everyone. I hate that you're gone. That you had to leave for it.*

Me too, I text back to Noah Michaelson.

Can I come see you over Thanksgiving break?

I brush my thumb over my screen. Even softer than the way I'd kissed him that day, not so long ago.

I know I'll have to go back there. There are things I'll have to say in front of people who won't want me to say them. There are things I need to say to Bean, even though nothing I say can or should erase what I did to her.

But I like the idea of seeing Noah outside that town, those people, and the events that have shaped our friendship so far.

What we can be, if we are somewhere else.

Okay.

I think about heroes. About the people we lay that mantle on. Superstars like Jay. How we let them uphold something greater than what we believe we have in ourselves and how, when they fail us, we fight back, and choose not to believe the truth about them. Because their failures are a reflection on us. It doesn't feel good, losing faith in someone.

I text Noah: *Who's your hero?*

His answer doesn't come for a while.

Streetlamps come on, challenging twilight with their soft glow.

Aunt Bea calls my name and I answer her with a mumbled, "Yeah?" but she doesn't say anything else, as if she just needed to check to make sure I am still here.

My mom, I guess. A pause. *What about yours?*

Noah's name comes to mind easily. So does Bean's. It feels, somehow, too early to admit it's them, though.

So I text, *Yeah. My mom, too.*

I stuff my phone in my pocket and think, as the door closes behind me, as I clutch the handle of my bag, walk down the hallway to my room, about being broken. Burning down.

About how much I hate the people who took my home away from me.

About how I hope, one day, to be able to hate myself a little less.

Because home isn't a sweeping view from a bluff, or the scent of cinnamon sugar in the air, or the crackling of a dry road under a horse's hooves.

Home is where you can live with yourself.

ACKNOWLEDGMENTS

I'M SO GRATEFUL TO all the friends and heroes who helped make this book a reality.

Thank you to my editor, Sarah Barley, who patiently steered this story from something that was more of a vague idea into what it is now. Her insights and patience are remarkable and I'm lucky to have her on my team. I'm grateful for designer Sarah Creech and art director Alison Donalty, who made this book look pretty; editorial director Erica Sussman, whose support of my work has been monumental; production editor Jon Howard, who catches my silly mistakes; and Heather Doss in sales, who is amazing at getting books into the world. Thank you to Jocelyn Davies, who stepped in to help put the final touches on this book. A huge thank-you to the rest of the team at HarperTeen who had a part in promoting this book and *Nobody But Us*. You are all awesome.

My writing career would be a disaster without the generous talents of my agent, Suzie Townsend. I'm so grateful for her guidance in all stages of writing and publishing. Thank you to the entire, very talented New Leaf Literary team: Joanna Volpe, Pouya Shabizan, Kathleen Ortiz, Danielle Barthel, Jaida Temperly, and David Caccavo. I appreciate everything each of you does.

To the YA writing community—aka the best writing community in the business—thank you for your support, your commiserations, your emails and tweets, your everything. In particular, love and gratitude go out to my dearest friends and YA Highway co-bloggers: Kate Hart, Kirsten Hubbard, Amy Lukavics, Kaitlin Ward, Stephanie Kuehn, Sumayyah Daud, Veronica Roth, Sarah Enni, Lee Bross, Leila Austin, Debra Driza, Emilia Plater, and Kristin Otts. *Alces Alces* forever.

And to all the readers and bloggers of YA: thank you for your passion.

My family always comes last in my acknowledgments, but first in real life. My thanks and love to Paul and my pixies for sharing this road with me and making every day precious beyond words.

AUTHOR'S NOTE

EVERY LAST PROMISE IS a work of fiction in its entirety.

But the story has been influenced by real-life events.

I didn't set out to write a book about rape. But as I read the news coverage of sexual assaults and their cover-ups in one small town—and then another and another—I kept wondering: What were these people thinking and feeling? How did those involved see themselves? And I really meant *everyone*. The perpetrators and the survivors, the friends, the families, the townspeople who supported one side or the other, the people who brought wrongdoings to light, and the ones who wanted it all to remain hidden.

I wanted to explore some of these points of view in *Every Last Promise*, to dig deeper behind the motivations of the people who can become caricatures in the media— and to grow my own empathy and understanding. And I couldn't stop thinking about those people who had seen or suspected something, but felt that they shouldn't—or couldn't—speak up.

And so, Kayla was born.

If you are or become the family or friend of a rape or sexual-assault victim, there are steps to take to be the best support possible. If someone tells you they've been raped, or if you know someone is a victim of sexual assault, follow these suggestions from RAINN and the Southern Arizona Center Against Sexual Assault:

1. First and foremost, believe the survivor. You might be the first and only person to ever say, "I believe you."
2. Reassure the survivor that the rape was not their fault. They might need to hear that what they experienced was a crime and not an act of sex.
3. Never forget that rape is not sex. It is a crime of power and a violent assault.
4. Acknowledge that the person who raped chose to rape and is the one responsible for not raping. Do not ask the survivor what they did "wrong" or tell them what they could have done differently. They are the victim of the crime.
5. Provide the number for the National Sexual Assault Hotline, 1-800-656-HOPE, or direct them to the National Sexual Assault Online Hotline, www.ohl.rainn.org/online, if they want to report the rape. Empower your friend or family member by being supportive and encouraging, but not pressuring them to act before they are ready. In addition to the rape culture and rape myths that discourage victims from reporting on a broader societal level, sexual assault victims

may be dealing with closer cultural pressures—like Bean vs. her small town—or even interfamily dynamics. Approximately two-thirds of rapes are committed by someone the victim knows, with almost 35 percent of juvenile rapes being perpetrated by a relative of the survivor.

6. Take care of yourself. Talk to someone at the National Sexual Assault Hotline about what you can do to be supportive, about how you feel, and about ways to cope and ways to stay healthy.

Ultimately, do your best to be a friend.
Survivors need friends.

With love and friendship,
Kristin